Peril on the Peninsula

An Alex Paige Travel Mystery

Theresa L. Carter

Molly,
I hope you enjoy my first "Paige" turner.

Love,
Theresa L. Carter

The Local Tourist

Copyright © 2022 by Theresa L. Carter

Published in the United States by The Local Tourist

thelocaltourist.com

First Edition

All rights reserved. No part of this book may be reproduced in any form, or by any means, electronic or mechanical, including photocopying, recording, or any information browsing, storage, or retrieval system, without permission in writing from the publisher, except for the use of brief quotations in a book review or as allowed by copyright law.

This is a work of fiction. Names, characters, businesses, places, events and incidents are the products of the author's imagination or are used fictitiously. Any resemblance to actual persons, living or dead, or actual events is purely coincidental.

ISBN 978-1-958187-25-8

Contents

1. Chapter 1 — 1
2. Chapter 2 — 14
3. Chapter 3 — 24
4. Chapter 4 — 38
5. Chapter 5 — 44
6. Chapter 6 — 53
7. Chapter 7 — 61
8. Chapter 8 — 71
9. Chapter 9 — 80
10. Chapter 10 — 90
11. Chapter 11 — 100
12. Chapter 12 — 110
13. Chapter 13 — 121
14. Chapter 14 — 132
15. Chapter 15 — 142
16. Chapter 16 — 150
17. Chapter 17 — 160
18. Chapter 18 — 170

19. Chapter 19	181
20. Chapter 20	190
21. Chapter 21	201
22. Chapter 22	210
23. Chapter 23	217
Author Note	229
Acknowledgments	231
About Theresa L. Carter	234

Chapter 1

Sunlight sparkled through the trees like fireflies. Alex opened the car windows. Pine. It smelled like pine. And dirt. And water. It wasn't the brine of the sea, but she could still smell Lake Michigan. Its vast expanse was like a homing beacon.

It was a late August afternoon. She'd followed the coast north from Chicago, taking her time to stop at each lighthouse she could find. Despite celebrating her 51st birthday just three months before, childlike wonder consumed her. It was no surprise, really; surviving breast cancer could do that for a person.

Alex tipped her head towards the window, the wind buffeting her short curls. Even that filled her with joy. In the past year, she'd left her condo only for medical treatments. She'd never been so lonely or isolated. Every time she saw her nurses, she'd begin a monologue that ran the entire four hours she sat in the chair. Those saints gracefully listened, replied when appropriate, and the following week would ask her about things she'd mentioned the week before.

They made the worst time of her life, if not enjoyable, at least bearable.

The only people she saw besides her medical team were her best friend Emily, her now-ex boyfriend Ben, and the couriers who dropped groceries at her door. While she was grateful that she could order whatever she wanted and it would simply show up, the isolation made her stir-crazy. Alex gravitated towards solitude, but for someone who traveled for a living, being stationary was stifling.

But she'd finished her treatments. She'd faced the beast and was cancer free. To celebrate, she accepted an invitation to visit a small town in Wisconsin's famous Door County. She was joining a select group of travel writers for a few days of exploration, research, and, if things were like they'd been before her diagnosis, outright pampering.

Alex was ready. Oh boy, was she ready.

As she neared her destination, occasionally she'd pass a sign planted next to the road. "Save our home. Say NO to Kaine's Course!" it pleaded. Her old instincts raised their eyebrows. *Could it be?* She'd ask. She'd be on the peninsula for three days, and she would learn as much as possible about the place in that short time. Her heart sped up. "Do I even remember how to do this?"

She squeezed the steering wheel and took a deep, calming breath. "Yes, you do, Alex," she muttered to herself. Then said it again, louder. She did this often.

Pep talks were how she'd gotten through the last year, and she knew they'd get her through the next few days.

Boutiques soon replaced the groves of birches and cypress and the cottages that overlooked the lake. She turned into a circular driveway and saw the red top of a lighthouse beyond the roof of a two-story lodge. The entrance was an impressive dark timbered A-frame. Although it was summer, she pictured it covered in snow, with garlands of lights strung across its front.

Alex pulled into a spot to the right of the entrance and turned off the car. She steeled herself. Took another calming breath. Got out, slung her laptop bag over her shoulder, pulled her carry-on out of the trunk and walked towards the front doors. She gripped the handle of her suitcase. "Pull it together," she said. "You can do this." Inhaling deeply, she lifted her head, rolled her shoulders back, and entered the historic inn.

She paused in the entry, her eyes adjusting to the dim lighting after the bright afternoon sunshine. Straight ahead was a wide staircase with curving banisters of dark polished wood, carved from logs and worn smooth from decades of use. The reception desk lined the wall to the right, and Alex walked over.

A statuesque young woman looked up. When she smiled around a mouthful of braces, it was obvious she was a teenager. The older Alex got, the younger everyone else appeared. *By the time I'm sixty, I'll think she's twelve*, she thought.

"Welcome to The Mast," the receptionist said. "Are you checking in?"

"Yes. My name's Alex Paige," she noted as she pulled out her driver's license and a credit card. "I'm one of the writers who's visiting this week." She reached down to scratch the ears of a fluffy fat cat that had padded over to rub against her calf. The white Persian turned its head so Alex could get the exact spot behind the ear; its face was so flat it looked like he'd run headlong into a wall. She stood up and brushed white fur off her hands.

"Ah - you're our first to arrive! And I see you've met Alvin."

Alex raised an eyebrow and smiled. "As in Alvin's Landing? Is he named for the town, or is the town named for him?"

The receptionist giggled. "He definitely likes to think the town is his, don't you?" she said to the cat. "Alvin here was a stray that kind of took over the place, so Evelyn, the owner, named him after her great-great-grandfather. Hold on, I've got something for you." She turned around and picked up one of several gift baskets arranged on the credenza. Alex could see an envelope with her name on it, a journal, a coffee mug, and a bag of chocolate-covered cherries, among other goodies nestled in the wicker.

"And the great-great-grandfather is who they named the town for," Alex confirmed, looking at the teenager's name tag. "Is that right, Lindsay?"

"Exactly! Landed here during a storm and never left. The whole story's on a USB drive in your basket." Lindsay placed two plastic cards in a sleeve and set it on the counter. "Here's your keys. You'll be on the second floor at the end of the hall." She leaned over and whispered, "You've got stairs to the beach next to your room; I think it's the best spot in the place!" Lindsay winked, then straightened up and continued in her official voice. "Your itinerary's in the basket as well, and the opening reception begins at six tonight in the Schooner Room." Lindsay pointed up the stairs. "It's right up there at the top. You can't miss it."

"Thank you. Will you be at the reception?"

"Oh no," she said. "I just man the desk. I guess I should say I woman it," she giggled again. *What a delightful young lady*, Alex thought. "But I'm sure I'll see you lots over the next few days. Enjoy your stay."

Before Alex turned around, a voice purred in her ear, "What's a fine specimen like you doing in a place like this?" She'd recognize that voice anywhere.

"William!" Alex spun around and hugged the gorgeous man behind her.

"What are you doing here?" he said.

"Well, hello to you, too! I decided last minute - as in yesterday. I wasn't sure how I'd feel."

"I'll forgive you for not telling me, then," he said. "I am SO glad to see you. Would you look at that hair! It's coming back thick. Very Cruella de Vil. Love it." William grabbed Alex's chin and turned her head left and right, like he was her grandmother making sure she looked healthy. Which, in a way, was exactly what he was doing. "It suits you."

Alex patted her curls, short and black and streaked with gray. She knew it wouldn't be long before she'd have a hard time taming them. That was just fine with her, since until two months ago she didn't know if her hair would ever grow back.

"Thank you, thank you. I'm getting used to it." The two grinned at each other like a couple of lovesick teenagers, although they were nothing of the sort. The first time Alex and William met had been four years before on a press trip on the Mississippi River. They hit it off immediately, mainly because they both had a crush on the same guy. William left Missouri with a phone number, and Alex had found a new friend.

"And look at you, Mister Oh-So-Rugged. Seems like campervan life still suits you."

William preened. He somehow made preening look natural, like it was the only appropriate response to compliments. "Yes, yes it does, doesn't it?" he said. "I tell you, though. I am ready for a few nights of de-luxe accommodations."

"You and me both," she said. Alex hoisted her gift basket. "Looks like they'll be taking care of us this week. After this past year, I am ready."

"I bet you are," he said, and turned to check in with Lindsay, stooping to pet Alvin first. "Well, hello there,

Mr. Fatty Flatty-Face! They didn't tell me a feline'd greet us. This day keeps getting better."

While Alex waited, she scoped out the lobby. A giant globe sat between shelves laden with leather-bound books and mariners' navigational tools. She recognized a sextant, a few telescopes, and several compasses. Lithographs of schooners and aged photos of the inn's early beginnings lined the walls. Leather couches and chairs studded with brass tacks sat in clusters designed for conversation. On the other side of the room, the gift shop displayed branded apparel, plus books on ship lore, how-to fishing and hunting guides, and marine-themed keepsakes. There were even a few ships-in-glass-bottles. The whole place felt like a throwback, what she imagined a seafarer's library would be. It was warm and charming, and she felt instantly at home.

William had just thanked Lindsay when a petite woman with wavy red hair and a sprinkle of freckles across her cheeks stormed into the lobby. The woman stopped abruptly, spinning to face a skinny man in a button-down plaid shirt. Alex thought he looked like someone trying simultaneously to be preppy and rugged. Neither worked.

The redhead jabbed a delicate finger at the man. "You knew," she seethed. Even from yards away, Alex could see the woman was seething. "You knew what he planned to do all along, didn't you?"

The man reached out, but the woman brushed his hands away.

"Evelyn," he said, "what did you think was going to happen? That he was going to plunk down all that money and not change a thing? This is an investment, hon. The inn needs to change."

"No, it does not. It is just fine the way it is," she said, each syllable clipped like her words were being transmitted by telegraph.

"Evelyn, Evelyn, c'mon. You know things can't stay the same," he whispered, putting his hands on her shoulders. This time, she let him. "You know this. I know you do."

The woman slumped and nodded slightly with her eyes fixed on the floor. William moved next to Alex. "Don't stare," he whispered. Alex turned her head away, realizing she was going to have to get used to being around people again.

Evelyn must have caught the movement with her peripheral vision, because she looked over. She visibly shook herself off, pasted a smile on her face, and walked the few steps towards them with her hand outstretched. "Hello there," she said. "You must be a couple of the writers here for the week."

Alex shifted her gift basket on her hip so she could take the proffered hand. "Hi, I'm Alex, and this is William."

"Oh, I'm sorry!" the woman laughed. "I should have seen you had your hands full. I'm Evelyn Dahl. My brother, Lars, and I own," she paused; "owned this inn and we're thrilled you'll be staying with us."

"If your lobby is any indication, we're going to love it here," William said.

Evelyn looked at the man with whom she'd been arguing, who was now standing next to her, with what seemed like vindication. He ignored the pointed glare and reached out his hand.

"Hi, I'm Nicholas Langley, but my friends call me Nick," he said, shaking their hands with the vigorous attention of a used car salesman. Or a politician. "I'm Village President." Of course you are, Alex thought. "More importantly, I'm engaged to this lovely woman and I can tell you she runs a tight ship," he said while draping his arm around the redhead. "Ba dum bum."

Evelyn's smile thinned. She bent down to pick up Alvin, using the movement to step gracefully away from her fiancé. "Lindsay, it looks like these are our first to arrive. I'm going to head to the marina, but I've got my radio; will you let me know when the rest of our writers check in?"

Lindsay nodded, and Evelyn turned back to Alex and William. "I'm sure Lindsay mentioned the itinerary's in your basket. My card's in there, too, so if you need anything during your stay, please don't hesitate to let me know."

She set Alvin on the back of a couch, turned around, and headed to the opposite corner of the room, walking under a driftwood sign carved with "This way to

The Rowdy Cormorant" and disappeared downstairs. The cat jumped down and padded after her, and Alex's eyes followed, noticing the marina through the floor-to-ceiling windows. Nick watched Evelyn, then he turned back and quickly shook Alex's and William's hands, although not quite as aggressively this time. "It was nice meeting you both. I'll be at the reception this evening, and I look forward to talking with you more." He slicked back his hair with his right hand and, to their surprise, turned and walked out the front door.

"Huh," William said. "I thought for sure he'd follow her."

"You and me both." They began walking towards the elevators. "Seems like this trip may be a little more interesting than normal."

"Oh, Alex, every trip with you is interesting."

William was Alex's travel writing buddy, and she especially looked forward to any press trip when she knew he'd be there. Knowing he'd be on this trip had influenced her decision to attend. That, and because if she didn't get out of the house soon, she'd pull out her very short hair and she didn't want to have to grow it all over again.

William specialized in outdoorsy adventures and wrote for the biggest national and airline publications. He traveled the country in his campervan, Bessie, named after his spunky grandmother. She'd been a rebel soul who hated being confined to one place. After she died, he quit his corporate job, bought a campervan, christened her for the woman who'd always inspired him, and never looked back. The life, as Alex said, suited him, and he had the freedom to indulge his passion for nature. His devotion to the great outdoors came through in beautiful, lyrical prose that made the reader feel like she was waking up to the same bubble-gum colored sunrise he did.

Small towns were Alex's area of expertise. She believed that every place, and every person, had a story, and she wanted to tell all of them. People opened up to her; it was a gift that meant her pieces always had that something extra. She'd begun her career as an investigative journalist and was making a name for herself when she realized she couldn't do it anymore. Uncovering corruption was worthy and necessary, and she knew that, but she was too much of an empath. It was destroying her soul.

After one last story that ended up in a conviction, but with no justice, she quit. She'd had a dream as a young girl to travel the country and tell its stories and decided that's exactly what she was going to do. It had been five years, and although she occasionally freelanced, she published most of her work on her own site. Alex had a fierce independent streak and wanted editorial control. Writing for herself had the added benefit of paying much better, and much more consistently.

Until last year.

"You really do look great," William said.

Alex smiled and thanked him. They got off the elevator on the second floor. "We've got a couple of hours before the reception," she said. "I'm going to tour the grounds. Want to join me?"

"I'd love to, but I've got to file a story," he looked at his watch, "within the next forty-five minutes. I'll text you when I'm done." He bussed her cheek and opened the door to his room.

"Sounds good. Have fun writing!" She walked to the end of the corridor and entered a spacious suite with a plush, king-sized bed, a couch and coffee table, a desk, and a wet bar, where she set down the basket. What grabbed her attention, though, were the picture windows and the glass door that led to a balcony. She stepped out and looked over the marina and its rows of mostly empty docks; the sail boats, speedboats, fishing boats, and yachts must be out for the day. Lake Michigan danced, the light reflecting on the ripples like fireworks. A tear slid down her cheek.

"I'm here," she thought. "I'm back."

This was going to be harder than she realized. More than once in the last year she thought she'd never be a travel writer again. The interminable treatments, the nausea, the parade of side effects that continued to pop up even now, two months after her last radiation - would she ever be truly done?

She decided it didn't matter if she was or wasn't, if she ever felt healthy, or strong, or like her old self. She knew she would never feel like her old self again.

And that was okay. Because, really, how could she?

Chapter 2

Alex added a touch of mascara, happy that she had eyelashes once more, even if they were a little thin. She grabbed her room key and cross-body bag containing her camera and her notebook. It was time to get to work.

She found the staircase Lindsay had mentioned next to her room and practically skipped down the flight. She flung the door open, crossed the sidewalk into the grass, and turned to face the back of the inn. A swath of grass ended where the marina began. Clusters of red, blue, and yellow Adirondack chairs reclining on the sandy beach beckoned, and Alex knew that's where she'd be watching the sunrise the next morning. She slipped off her white canvas tennies and felt the cold silkiness of the grass. It was damp; beads of water clung to the blades, like a sprinkler had recently been running. She walked towards the shore. Grass became dunes became beach, and Alex spontaneously grinned. Sand clung to her feet and she rinsed them off in the gently lapping water. To her left were a couple of fire rings filled with charred logs and, behind them in the grass, an outdoor bar where a young man stocked beer and liquor for the evening. Alex stopped to talk to him for a moment. "What time do you open?"

"Five," he said. "We've got live music starting at five-thirty. A local singer-songwriter duo from Chicago who play here every summer. They're great - you should come by."

"If I can, I will," she said, although she knew she probably wouldn't be able to. These press trips were always go-go-go and they squeezed the itineraries full of activities. Maybe she could find a way. It would provide great local color.

She resumed walking until she arrived at the marina. It was a decent size, but small compared to the harbor she could see from her condo in Chicago. That marina would practically swallow the whole town of Alvin's Landing, as would some of the yachts. At the base of the marina, she saw a sign for the Rowdy Cormorant on a cabin connected to the inn by an open breezeway. A little further, a squat building with large picture windows faced the marina. Between the two sat an old fishing shack, its white-washed boards flaking paint like dandruff. A sign advertised Live Bait. The shack looked like it had been there since the 1800s, and Alex realized it just may have been. It contrasted with the modern metallic docks, which were obviously new; it didn't look like they'd been through even one season.

She started making her way toward the shack, stopping to take pictures for her site and social media. She framed the back of the inn, the beach, and the marina. When she reached the dock, she put her canvas tennies back on and walked silently on their rubber soles. A woman sat on a bench facing the water, her face in her hands. The fat white cat from the lobby sat at the woman's feet, one paw on a freckled shin. Before Alex could decide whether to turn around or keep heading towards the obviously distraught redhead, Evelyn lifted her head, recognizing the journalist. Evelyn wiped her face and scooped up Alvin, who turned in a circle before settling in with his head on his paws. He covered Evelyn's lap entirely. "Hi Alex; did you find your room okay?"

"Yes, and it's beautiful, thank you. I love the balcony. May I?" Alex asked, and when Evelyn nodded, she sat down. "Makes me wish I could sit there all day, but I know we've got a lot to see."

"Sue's definitely got you busy while you're here."

Alex reached over to scratch Alvin behind the ears. "This is quite some place," she said. "How long has it been in your family?"

"Forever," Evelyn said. "My great-great-grandfather built that fishing shack in 1898. Sometimes I can't believe it's still standing." She smiled, but it quickly disappeared. "And now we're going to lose it all," she murmured.

Alex gave Evelyn a sideways glance. The reporter in her wanted to ask. She didn't.

Evelyn tipped her head back to get the full force of the sun on her face. She visibly calmed herself, then looked at Alex, specifically at her hair. "You're a survivor?"

"That obvious, huh?"

"I recognize the curls." Evelyn ran her fingers through her full head of red waves. "It comes back. It'll take some time, but it comes back."

"Was yours always red?" Alex asked.

"Yes, but after chemo it turned white and then had streaks of brown, blonde, and red. I felt like a calico."

"I know what you mean. William said I look like Cruella de Vil. Personally, I'm thinking more bride of Frankenstein."

Evelyn snorted, startling the cat. Alvin jumped down and stalked off in a huff. The two survivors laughed. "How long has it been?" Alex asked.

"Six years."

"Wow. You must have been pretty young."

"I was thirty-one, so yes," Evelyn said, then glanced at Alex. "You're young yourself."

Alex laughed. "Fifty-one, thank you very much. If I had to get it, I'm grateful it happened when my body was still pretty strong. Now I'm determined it always will be."

Evelyn scooted back and stretched out her legs, crossing them at the ankles. She hugged her chest. "I know what you mean. It was awful, the worst experience of my life, but at least one good thing came out of it."

"Oh?" Alex prompted.

"This. That I'm here. I'd been living the high life in the big city, but when I got that diagnosis, the only place I wanted to be was here. It's home."

Alex could hear the sadness in Evelyn's voice. "Tell me about it," she said. "Makes you realize what's important."

"It sure does. And this place—the inn, the marina, Alvin's Landing, all of it—this is the most important thing in the world to me." Evelyn's eyes glistened. She sat forward and put her head in her hands. "I don't know what I'm going to do."

Alex waited. "What happened?" she finally asked, softly.

"Honestly? I don't know. We had a terrible storm last winter that destroyed the docks and ripped off the roof on one wing. That meant all new docks and a whole new roof, but we should have had enough to cover it," Evelyn said, then forced a smile. "Enough about that. You're not here to listen to my problems."

"I do have one question," Alex said. "As I was driving in, I saw signs about Kaine's Course. Would that be Trevor Kaine?"

Evelyn's head snapped towards her. "You know him?"

"Oh, yes. I know him," Alex said, and stopped. She didn't want to talk about Kaine and the profound impact he'd had on her life.

"Well then, what's happening here won't surprise you." Evelyn paused.

Alex waited. She knew that silence created a vacuum that needed to be filled, and while she was somewhat surprised that Evelyn was being so open with her, especially considering she was there, in part, to learn about the wonders of this woman's family business, Alex also knew her gift. People talked to her. They always had. Cashiers, fellow commuters, soon-to-be-indicted felons. They all talked to her. After being isolated from all but a few of those closest to her and her medical team for the past year, Alex was relieved to know she still had that something, whatever it was, that inspired people to confide in her, even when they knew she was a writer.

"After the expenses from the roof and the docks, we were going to lose the inn," Evelyn continued. "The marina. Everything. Then he shows up.

"Nick brought him in. He'd worked with him in Chicago and said Kaine was the answer to all my problems. I knew of him; he'd been a summer local for years. But then I guess he decided Chicago wasn't enough; he needed a piece of this." She gestured with her left arm and then brought her hand back and twisted her engagement ring. "He gave us an offer we couldn't refuse," Evelyn said wryly, then grimaced and stared out at the old fishing shack. "We signed the papers this morning. Trevor Kaine now owns The Mast and everything that comes with it."

Oh no, Alex thought. Now she understood the argument between Evelyn and Nick in the lobby. She knew Kaine. She knew that if he had his way, what she saw now, everything that made this place comfortable and inviting, would disappear.

"I'm so sorry," Alex said. "What's the deal with the signs about a course?"

"Golf course. See that forest? Those bluffs? All of that natural beauty?" Evelyn pointed to the undeveloped land on the other side of the marina. "He wants to turn it into a golf course." The disgust rolled off of her like steam. "And guess where he wants to put the pro shop?"

Alex realized immediately. "The fishing shack."

"Yep. You'll see the plans tonight. He unveiled them this morning. After we signed the paperwork, of course."

"Can you back out?"

"And do what? No. The banks won't give us a loan and no other investors are showing up." Evelyn sounded defeated. "And Nick knew. He knew all along." She held out her hand and looked at her ring. The reflection of the sun off the diamond practically blinded Alex. It didn't suit Evelyn in the slightest. "He's not who I thought he was."

"Men," Alex commiserated.

Evelyn raised her eyebrows. "Spoken like someone who knows. You single?"

"I am now. Let's just say he wasn't who I thought he was, either." Alex sighed. "You discover a lot about someone when you go through something traumatic, and I discovered I didn't really like him, and I certainly didn't like who I was with him."

"Good for you."

"Thanks." Alex paused. "I realized—and I know you've probably felt this, too—that you don't know what's going to happen from one moment to the next, so I darn well better choose what I do with each moment wisely. There was no way I was going to spend another moment with someone I didn't like or respect, and who certainly didn't respect me. I was a trophy, and the way Ben acted through my treatment?" Alex rolled her eyes. "He thought he was so noble, insisting on driving me to treatments, buying flowers weekly even though I told him the scent made me sick because of the chemo.

"Then he told me I'd be beautiful again once my hair grew back."

Evelyn gasped. "He actually said that?"

"Uh, huh. I looked at him straight on and said, 'I'm beautiful now. Thank you for everything, but we're through.'"

Evelyn inhaled. "How'd he take that?"

"Let's just say he's persistent." Alex glanced at Evelyn. She wondered if the other woman was considering how Nick would take a similar goodbye.

"I'm half afraid he's going to show up here. Even though it's been a couple months, he hasn't quite gotten the message."

"Men," they said together.

They smiled at each other. "I probably shouldn't have told you all that, considering what you do," Evelyn said, "but for some reason, I trust you."

"I'm glad you did. And don't worry. I'm a happy writer." Inside, though, Alex was scheming. She knew Trevor Kaine and what he was capable of, and she was going to do everything she could to help save the Mast. Alex didn't know what that was, but she'd put him down once. She could do it again.

Alex's phone vibrated and she looked at the screen. *How's Alvin's Landing?* "Speak of the devil."

"You're kidding, really?" Evelyn asked.

"He's like Beetlejuice. Don't say his name three times."

"Sounds like you've got your very own Voldemort."

Alex laughed. "Ha! He's not quite that bad, but you know how I said he was persistent?" She waved the phone and it buzzed again. "Oh, come on! You've got to be kidding me."

Please stop, she typed, but before sending, realized the second message wasn't from her ex. *It's time to get ready!*

"Saved by the William."

Evelyn raised her eyebrows.

"He's letting me know it's time to clean up for the reception. He must've gotten his story filed." Alex quickly replied *On my way* and stood up. "It was really great talking with you."

"You, too. I think I needed it."

"It would be a wonder if you didn't," Alex said. "I'm sorry about what you're going through."

Evelyn's eyes swept across the marina, landing on the fishing shack. "Thanks. Me, too," she said softly. "Well, I'm for damn sure going to make sure I enjoy it while I can, which means enough moping and time for me to get ready as well." Evelyn walked towards the front of the inn, and Alex walked back along the beach to her corner.

"There you are!"

Alex looked up to see William leaning on his balcony. "Hurry and get changed so we can grab a drink."

"Yes, dear," she grinned.

As Alex changed into something more appropriate for a welcoming reception, her determination to help Evelyn grew. This was Trevor Kaine, and she knew that whatever he had planned would not be good.

Chapter 3

"You're kidding. Trevor Kaine is here? He bought this place?" William asked.

"Yes, and you know and I know there's something hinky in the contract."

"Of course there is. It's Trevor Kaine." He took a sip of his beer. "Think he'll recognize you?"

"I don't think so. I look a little different now," she said, patting her hair. "And besides, I could barely get past his gatekeeper and he never deigned to give me anything but a phone interview. All my in-person investigating was with people he'd damaged, hurt, or outright ruined. The rest was contracts, etc. FOIA was definitely my friend." As an investigative journalist, Alex had frequently requested filings through the Freedom of Information Act.

"What a slog."

"You got that right. I kind of miss it, though."

William put his beer down and looked at her like she'd lost her mind. "Really? You miss spending hours and hours trying to find that one little detail that'll 'throw the book at 'em,' as they say?"

"Sometimes. It felt great to know that what I was doing was helping people."

"A, you help people now and B, at what cost? I didn't know you then, but from what you've said, you were miserable. Not eating, not sleeping, and look—you ended up with someone like—"

"Don't say his name! You'll conjure him. He's already texted me once today and apparently knows I'm here," she grimaced. "I wish he'd get the hint and leave me alone."

William shook his head. "You know as well as I do that is not going to happen. Maybe you can sic Harriet on him."

Alex burst out laughing. "Now that's an idea! She's been after him for years. Who knows? They might be very happy together."

He looked sideways at her. "You know she's going to be here, right?"

"What? No. Seriously? My first trip back and not only is Kaine involved, she's going to be here, too." Alex sipped her beer and wiped a bit of foam from her upper lip. "Thank goodness you're here. You're going to keep me in line, right?"

"Heck no. I'm going to be riling you up."

Alex clinked her glass to his. "That's why I love you."

They were sitting at the bar. At four-thirty in the afternoon, the Rowdy Cormorant was anything but.

When they were on press trips together, it was their habit to meet for a drink before the madness began. They knew this would most likely be the only time they'd have together, because once the tour started, the next few days would be all about the destination. There would be some opportunities to chat, but mostly, they focused entirely on work.

Before they realized it, more than an hour had passed and they were going to be late to the reception. They finished their now-lukewarm pints and exited the lounge, following the path that paralleled the marina. A group of tourists piled out of a tour boat named Amelia and walked towards the inn.

"Oh, my," William said. "Would you look at that?"

"How could I not?"

They stopped to appreciate a tall, wide-shouldered, scruffy-faced, lantern-jawed man wiping down the boat. The man looked up at them and nodded, and then he gazed beyond them and smiled thinly at a brunette walking in his direction.

"Hey, Juke," they heard her say. "Ready for tomorrow?"

"Of course. You sure we should still do it with today's news?" His voice was a deep rumble that resonated in Alex's very core. She and William had to keep walking, so they couldn't continue eavesdropping.

"I think he's our tour guide tomorrow," Alex said.

"I certainly hope so," William said as he craned his neck to continue staring.

Alex nudged him and he faced forward. "I don't. We won't hear a thing he says. Now that is one cool drink of—"

"Um-hmm. You said it."

They entered the inn and walked upstairs to the Schooner Room. It was smaller and more intimate than Alex expected, but it overlooked the marina and the A-frame provided soaring windows. The sun wouldn't set for another couple of hours and it was a beautiful summer evening. Although they were only five minutes past the reception's start time, it was already in full swing. She saw Evelyn talking with Jackie, a writer Alex knew who was based out of Seattle, and a couple of people she didn't recognize. Near the windows, Nick rested his elbow on the bar while a man wearing a slick suit ordered a drink. The man's back may have been to her, but Alex didn't need to see his face. She'd know Trevor Kaine anywhere.

And there was Harriet, right at Kaine's other side, shrugging her heavy purse up over her shoulder.

"Great. Her. And of course she's talking to him." Alex waited until Nick and Kaine, followed closely by Harriet, moved to a high-top, one of several standing in front of the windows. When it was clear, she and William walked to the bar and each ordered an Old Fashioned.

"When in Wisconsin," they cheered.

Over the rim of her glass, Alex observed the two men ignoring Harriet, who then noticed someone else was actually paying attention to her. "Incoming," Alex warned.

William turned around. Took a slow sip of his Old Fashioned. "Oh. Hello, Harriet."

"Hello," Alex said to her as well. "How are you?"

"Alexis. Bill." She slurped her white wine. "I see you two are starting with the strong stuff."

Alex tensed and William gently gripped the back of her arm, a warning to let it go.

Her name was Alex. Not Alexis, not Alexandra, not Alexa. Alex. William was William. Not Bill, and never, ever Billy.

As Alex had done every other time, she ignored it.

"We figured we'd try their specialty," Alex replied, "since we're here as their guests and all."

"Well, good for you if you can handle it. You know how these trips are, and I wouldn't want you to be worn out after your first night." Harriet paused and looked directly at Alex's chest. "Especially with what you've been through."

William jumped in before Alex could respond. "Thank you so much for your concern, Harriet." He dripped saccharin, but his sarcasm was unmistakable.

Alex took his cue, refusing to engage, and looked over Harriet's shoulder. "Oh, William, look. It's Jackie. I haven't seen her in ages. Shall we?" She steered him away. "Enjoy your wine, Harriet," she said over her shoulder.

William leaned in. "Breathe," he said under his breath as they walked.

"I am. I just wasn't ready to deal with—that—yet. Let's go see what Jackie's been up to."

Jackie tipped her glass of bubbly to Alex and William as they approached. "Well, hello, you two! Long time no see." Jackie turned to the others at the table with her. "Heather, Greg, meet Alex and William." The four shook hands.

While they talked, a passing server offered blackened whitefish wrapped in phyllo dough with heirloom tomatoes and crispy basil, shadowed by another wielding a tray of crostini topped with medium-rare steak, creamy brie, and cherry compote. The hi-top was quickly littered with crumpled napkins. As the writers talked, Alex watched Evelyn's fiancé work the room, parading like an arrogant A-lister on the red carpet. William could give him a lesson or two in preening, she thought.

A singular *ting* of a knife tapping a glass cut their conversation short, drawing their attention to the group standing at the windows. Alex recognized the woman who'd been talking to the tour boat captain that afternoon, although she'd changed out of her casual clothes into something more formal. Evelyn had changed, too, and she looked dazzling. Nick couldn't stop staring at her. Her emerald green pantsuit brought out her eyes and made her red hair even more vibrant. She looked distinctly uncomfortable, focusing on the floor with her arms crossed over her chest. She stood in the middle, with the other woman and Nick on one side and two men on the other.

Alex glared at the man closest to Evelyn with revulsion. His tailor-made navy suit made his girth look like it was more muscle than the fat she knew he carried, and he wore a silk shirt open at the neck, revealing a gold chain. A gold chain? Really? Kaine was even more of a cliché than she remembered. He towered over the nervous-looking man next to him, who kept looking at him like a puppy seeking approval. With his slight build, red hair, and freckles, this had to be Evelyn's brother, Lars.

Alex studied the dynamics of this odd group. Maybe it was her months of relative isolation while she took chemotherapy, but she was now even more attuned to the interplay between others. She'd always been empathetic, absorbing the feelings of those around her, which was why she had stopped being an investigative reporter, but now it was like her senses were on high alert. Alex assumed the woman at the end was Sue, the tourism director. She looked nervous. Nick looked smug. Evelyn looked like she wanted to scream or cry or both.

Standing to one side of the group was a woman holding a stack of folders to her torso, which was simultaneously lean and voluptuous. She looked familiar, but this was a woman she'd remember. She was stunning, in a Barbie-doll kind of way. Chocolate pencil skirt, beige silk camisole topped with a flowing olive-green kimono, stiletto heels, and eyelashes that were obviously not original equipment. Blond chunky curls pulled into a half-up, half-down, intentionally messy do that Alex knew took hours to put together. She touched her short curls; even when her hair was the same length as the blonde's, she couldn't invest that much time styling it. She'd planned on it, the last week before she shaved her head to prevent the trauma of it disappearing, clump by clump, but there were other things that were far more important to her, like baking cookies and spending time with friends and family. Or reading. Or writing. Or anything, really.

Alex felt a vague dislike for the woman, and she instantly admonished herself. She could be a perfectly lovely person, she thought. Alex knew she was being catty.

"Rawr," said William. Apparently, so did he.

"I know. I'm trying not to judge."

"Succeeding?"

"Trying."

Harriet glared at them from the next table over and shushed them. They smiled at her, then turned to face the row of people standing with their backs to the windows.

Once the brunette who'd tapped the glass with the knife had everyone's attention, she smiled at the room, putting the utensil on a passing tray and raising her glass. "Hello, and welcome to Alvin's Landing and

The Mast. I'm Sue Morris. As you know from our correspondence, I'm the director of our tourism board. It's nice to meet you all in person, and I want to extend my sincere thanks for visiting our home, our piece of peninsular paradise."

Alex gave William a sideways glance. "Peninsular paradise," they mouthed, grinning. There was nothing like a tourism professional selling a destination.

"I'll be with you the next few days, so I won't take up too much of your time tonight. I did, however, want to introduce you to a few people." Sue gestured to her left. "This is Nicholas Langley, our village president, and next to him is Evelyn Dahl, whom some of you have already met. At the end is her brother Lars. Their great-great-grandfather built The Mast. You could say it's in their blood.

"In between those two is Trevor Kaine. Mr. Kaine's from Chicago, but he's been spending his summers with us for ages, haven't you?"

The man nodded and put his hand on Evelyn's shoulder. She visibly bristled. Alex involuntarily focused on the signet ring circling his middle finger. The stone was bigger than the key card to her room. "I sure have, Sue," Kaine said. "Alvin's Landing is really something special, and we're about to make it even more special."

He put his other hand on Lars' shoulder, like he was laying claim to the siblings. "What these two have done with their little family business is wonderful, but I'm here to bring this piece of history into the twenty-first century."

Evelyn finally looked up and the stare she directed at the confident man with his slicked-back hair should have turned him to stone. Alex could understand that reaction. *Little family business* exuded condescension and derision. Par for the course with Trevor Kaine.

"What Lars and Evelyn have here is a quaint inn, but in the years I've been coming here, I've seen its potential. I've seen the potential of this whole county." He removed his hand from Evelyn's shoulder and snapped his fingers. One of the servers who'd been passing out appetizers jumped over with a remote control and a glass of sparkling rosé. "While you're here, you folks are going to be treated to some of the most beautiful landscapes and views you've ever seen. You'll also get an excellent taste—and I mean that literally—of the best food north of Chicago."

Kaine grabbed the drink with one hand and the remote with the other. He clicked a button and a screen dropped from the ceiling behind him.

"Yes," Sue jumped in during the break in his monologue as he swallowed. "We've put together an incredible itinerary—"

"But I believe," Kaine continued, as if she hadn't spoken, "that The Mast can be so much more. Alvin's Landing deserves so much more." Kaine took another sip of wine before continuing. "And I should know, since I've built some of the most successful developments in Chicago and the Midwest."

Alex choked on her drink, but Kaine didn't notice.

"If the serving staff could leave the room, please, I'll show you the bright future I've planned for this—what'd you call it, Sue?—peninsular paradise." He walked to the bar, refilled his wine, and pointed the remote at the same server who'd given it to him. "You. Dim the lights on your way out." She did as asked without acknowledging she'd heard him and slipped out the door.

"Ladies and gents, I present to you Kaine Resort and Spa."

Drone footage and renderings depicting Trevor Kaine's vision of what he believed Alvin's Landing "deserved" filled the screen. The comfortable inn, with its lodge-like feel, would become a white-washed resort. An infinity pool would replace the lawn and fire pits; the Rowdy Cormorant would no longer welcome locals as well as tourists and instead become a piano bar specializing in twenty-dollar martinis, ten-dollar craft beers, and shared plates that weren't big enough for one person, let alone two. There would be a luxurious spa with a menu of the most exclusive treatments. Gone would be the shack that still provided bait to the working anglers who docked at the marina. Gone would be the working anglers, their boats replaced by obnoxious yachts with names like *Diamond Destiny* and *Liquid Serenity*. Lars watched with avaricious glee, glancing between Kaine and the screen. Evelyn looked like she was going to be sick.

It took eleven minutes to detail the plans Kaine had for the inn, which were bad enough. Then, for the next nine, the video explained why there would no longer be a fishing shack; he was replacing it with a pro shop and a nineteenth hole—a pro shop and a nineteenth hole because he planned to turn the adjoining Reserve into a golf course.

William gripped Alex's hand. This was the opposite of what a place like Alvin's Landing should be. Kaine was going to make this comfortable getaway into one more cookie-cutter resort that catered to the one-percenters.

The lights went up and Kaine waited expectantly for applause. Four people clapped: Nick, Lars, and Harriet, of course, plus the Barbie in the shadows, who somehow managed to shift the folders she carried gracefully. *I would have dropped everything*, Alex thought, and realized she might be a tiny bit envious of the woman. Might be? Certainly.

"Mr. Kaine," Harriet gushed. "What marvelous plans you have. I can't wait to share the news."

"Deborah will get you all the details before you leave at the end of the week, right, Deborah?"

The blonde nodded. "Absolutely, Mr. Kaine."

Harriet tittered. "How exciting!" then looked around the room, lingering on the solid log beams that supported the A-frame. "Modernizing this place is going to make all the difference. I'd love to sit down with you and learn more about your plans."

Oh my word, Alex thought. Harriet was actually trying to flirt with the man.

William squeezed her fingers again. "She's not worth it," he muttered under his breath.

Kaine glanced at them, peeved that everyone wasn't as rapt as Harriet, and then responded to his newest fan. "I'm unavailable this week, but I'm sure Nick can spare some time for you, right, Nick?"

Nick, who'd been quiet during the presentation, nodded. "It would be my pleasure. Harriet, right? Don't you focus on luxury destinations?"

"Oh, yes. Finding only the best of the best is my specialty."

"Perfect," he said. "After we finish up here, let's set a time." Nick turned to Kaine. "You've got something else to tell them, don't you?"

"Yes, I do. Thanks for the pitch," Kaine replied, acting like he was catching a football before glancing at the tourism director. "Sue, I know you've got a tour of the Reserve set up for tomorrow morning. I decided that's the perfect opportunity to show everyone how we're capitalizing on the natural beauty of the park to create the premier golf course in the country."

He looked directly at Harriet. "You're going to love it."

Harriet beamed. Nick smirked. Sue and Evelyn simmered. Lars practically drooled. The rest stared in stunned silence.

During Kaine's presentation, the staff had set up a buffet on the terrace and put place settings on the outside tables. Evelyn invited everyone to eat and conversation gradually returned. Alex heard snippets here and there. "A golf course?" "But that shack is so charming." "I thought the lobby looked great." She was glad to hear she wasn't the only one appalled by the direction Kaine's investment would take The Mast.

She was also glad he didn't recognize her, not that, as she told William, she thought he would. It had been years since she'd sat in the back of the courtroom during his trial and conviction for fraud. During his testimony, the megalomaniac had even made eye contact with her and winked, obviously not realizing that she was Alex Paige, the journalist who had unearthed his scheme to defraud investors in his supposedly luxurious high-rise condominiums. Shortcuts and cheap materials would have ensured the building's collapse if she hadn't discovered that he was pocketing the difference between his invoices and the actual purchase orders.

Her investigation thwarted Kaine's plans to replace brownstones housing independent restaurants, retail shops, and bars with condos and parking garages. Fortunately, although she couldn't save the historic brownstones, Alex exposed Kaine's treachery before construction could begin, so only livelihoods, instead of lives, were lost.

Chapter 4

One of those livelihoods was Coda. The club had been in the same underground spot for years and Alex lost count of the number of times she'd taken the bus home at two in the morning after listening to the top jazz and blues musicians in the country.

She remembered the night six years ago when she learned that her favorite hangout, as well as all the other small businesses on the block, were under threat.

Alex had been gone for a month on an assignment investigating an embezzling ring in the southern part of the state. Seeing how those politicians had betrayed their constituents affected her deeply, and she knew she couldn't pursue those types of stories for much longer. Alex tasted bile just thinking about it and she needed a distraction or she'd never get to sleep. She finished unpacking and, even though it wasn't quite dusk and the band didn't start until the sun went down, she left her Lincoln Park condo and took a bus to the club. She found Georgia, Coda's owner, sitting hunched over the bar and swirling a rocks glass of brown liquor, staring at the whisky as it spun in circles around a large ball of clear ice.

"Grab a drink while you can," Georgia said, her voice husky from decades of smoke-filled rooms.

Alex sat next to her. "What's up?"

"They won't renew the lease. They've sold the building." Georgia nodded to the bartender and then tilted her head at Alex. "Get her one of these," she said.

"How long have you got?"

"Two months."

"So soon?" The bartender set a scotch in front of Alex and she took a drink. Smooth. Smoky. Georgia's drinking the good stuff, she thought. Things must be really bad.

"Yep."

"Can you open somewhere else?"

"Here? In Chicago? No. It's too expensive and the lawyers wiped me out." Georgia waved at the liquor lined up in rows on the mahogany bar. "What you see on those shelves is basically all I've got left."

"What are you going to do?" Alex asked.

"Head back home, I 'spose, although I haven't been there much in the past thirty years. My grandson knows a place I can play." Georgia swiveled on her barstool to face the stage at the back of the room. The band, normally keyed up before their gig, looked as despondent as Georgia. "I'll lose my band, and that sucks. These guys are the best."

They were pros, though, and they rallied when the lights went down. It was one of the best nights of music they'd had. Alex was determined to do what she could to save such a special place.

Unfortunately, proving what Kaine was up to took too long and the entire block, including Coda, was demolished. She did, however, feed the information about the payoffs and underhanded transactions to people who could actually do something about them.

Kaine was out of prison within nine months and was back wheeling and dealing. By then, Alex had moved on. Right after the trial, she turned in her press badge and started her new career as a travel writer. She was much happier, although she sometimes missed the thrill of the chase, of bringing down the bad guys.

And now here he was, ready to destroy another special place. Alex felt like Sisyphus, but she was determined to find out what, exactly, was happening. She knew there was something shady, not only because Kaine was involved, but because an aura of greed surrounded Nick and Lars like smog blanketing a factory-filled valley.

"Yoo-hoo, you here?" William moved in front to block her view of the men standing by the windows. The trio had barely moved four feet from the bar the entire night.

She pulled her gaze towards her friend. "Yeah, sorry. Just thinking about, you know," and she pointed her chin at Kaine et al.

"Have I told you lately how good you look?" he asked.

Alex grinned. William was one of a kind. "Thank you, dear man." She turned around and crooked her elbow. "I think it's time for us to learn more about Rowdy Cormorant since we didn't get much of a taste earlier, don't you?"

He put his arm through hers. "Lead on, Lady Macduff."

Alex wanted to say goodnight to Evelyn but didn't see her. Sue, however, was talking to Harriet near the doors. "Bye, Sue," she said as they neared the tourism director. "See you in the morning."

"Great. I'll be in the lobby at 7:30," Sue replied and hurried down the stairs.

"Bye, Bill and Alexis. Don't be late. You wouldn't want to miss any of the tour," Harriet said in a voice designed for others to overhear.

Enough. Alex stopped in her tracks and turned to face her. "His name is William," she clipped, and Harriet's chin dropped. "My name is Alex. Period."

Alex whipped around and headed to the lobby, refusing to look back. She could hear William behind her. He didn't say a word. Simply followed her.

They reached the bottom of the stairs and she turned tightly, controlling her movements lest she fly out of control. She squeezed her eyes shut, breathed deeply, and opened them to look at her friend with embarrassed frustration. "I know I shouldn't let her get to me, but I've had to put up with that woman and her condescension and her belittling since my very first press trip. She knows darn well what our names are, and she intentionally changes them to suit whatever agenda she has."

"I know," William said calmly.

Alex sank into one of the tufted leather couches across from the globe and pictured herself circumnavigating, flying high above the drama below. "Ever since my diagnosis, I've thought so much about who I am and what I want and what's important to me, and part of that is knowing that I can't let people like her walk all over me."

"I understand, but she's insignificant. She doesn't deserve your attention, let alone your ire."

"I know. I know. I know." Alex ran her fingers through her short hair. She still wasn't used to its length, or lack thereof, but at least it was growing back. "Gawd, she gets to me, though."

William sat sideways on the couch so he could face her and took her hands in his. "Alex, you are the strongest woman—person—I know. What you've been through in the past year is enough to fell anyone." He took a deep breath.

"I also know you have an intense sense of right and wrong, and to see Kaine, that poster child for greed, here, of all places, has to be too much. Throw Miss 'I Only Highlight The Best Of The Best,'" and here William gagged, which made Alex smile, "into the mix and I'm surprised you didn't start punching."

Alex inhaled to speak.

"But... " he put his finger on her lips to stop her. "But I haven't seen you in a year and a half, and you look great, and I look great, and I hear there's supposed to be a great jazz band less than five minutes away, and maybe that oh-so-fine boat captain will be there, and if he is and you make me miss him or the music because you want to go all Indignant Defender of the Wronged on me, then I may not speak to you again the rest of the week."

By the time he was done, Alex was laughing and put her hands up in surrender. "Fine, fine. You win, oh wise one."

William crooked his arm this time and she snaked hers through. "Promise you'll behave?" he asked.

"Not on your life. Now stop badgering me. I think I hear a sax calling my name."

Chapter 5

Alex stopped so suddenly that William bumped into her. "What?" he asked.

"It can't be," she said with awe.

"What is it? Is something wrong?"

"No, something's right! I'd know that voice anywhere. It's Georgia Brannigan."

"Of Coda-fame? That Georgia?" Any time William came to Chicago, Alex bemoaned she couldn't take him to her favorite club.

"Yes!" She grabbed his hand and pulled him towards the door. She yanked it open and Georgia's husky tones and exuberant piano playing blasted her in the face. She felt indescribable joy. It had been six years since she'd heard that music, six long years. She'd often wondered what happened to Georgia after the building her club had occupied for decades was demolished, but with Alex's new travel writing career, and then cancer, she never looked her up.

Alex found two seats at the bar and they bellied up. She was a bar person. Any time she traveled, she wanted to find the local hangout because that's where, logically, she'd meet the locals. She turned to smile at the person next to her and realized it was Evelyn. "Hi, Evelyn! You've got Georgia Brannigan here? That is amazing."

Evelyn, who'd been staring into her cocktail, looked up and smiled. "You know Georgia? Small world."

"Yeah," William agreed. "What are the odds?"

Alex craned to see the band, tapping her foot as the music buffeted her like a Midwestern thunderstorm. "Actually, they're pretty good. This area's a big feeder market for Chicago, and vice versa. They come here to get away from the chaos of the city, and people from here go there to get a little more excitement."

Evelyn was nodding her head. "Exactly. I went to school in Evanston and spent my first years in hospitality in downtown Chicago. I used to go to Georgia's club any chance I could."

"Coda?" Alex asked with surprise, and Evelyn nodded. "Seriously? We probably passed each other on the way to the bathroom, or at the bar. That was my favorite hangout when I was reporting."

"Small world," Evelyn said again.

"How'd she end up here?"

Evelyn grinned. "Believe it or not, she's from here. After she lost her club, she came back home. As soon as I found out, I scooped her up before anybody else could." Her smile faded. "Now I'm afraid she's going to lose another one, and it's all my fault."

Alex looked at her with alarm. "How could it be your fault, Evelyn? It's nobody's fault but that greedy SOB's."

Evelyn shook her head. "She lost her Chicago club because of him. I didn't know it was Kaine, but it doesn't matter." Her voice softened to a whisper, and Alex could barely hear her over the music. "I just didn't know what else I could do. It was the only way to save this place, but it's not saving it at all."

"You can't blame yourself for grasping at what you thought was a lifeline," Alex said.

William, who'd been silent, spoke up. "She's right, you know." He paused. "How did Kaine get involved in the first place?"

Evelyn's lips compressed into a thin, angry line. "That's a long story." The front door opened and her head swiveled to the entrance; her eyes burned at the man who'd entered. "One that involves him." She put her hands on the bar and stared at her left ring finger, then decisively removed the gaudy diamond ring. "Please excuse me for a moment."

Alex and William watched Evelyn stride purposefully towards Nick. At first he smiled, but then he seemed to realize he was in big trouble. He reached his hand out to her. She turned it over and put the ring in his palm.

Nick looked at it in disbelief. "You can't be serious!" he sputtered. "Because of him? Because I brought in someone who could save this dump?" he gestured wildly.

"Uh-oh," Alex and William said together.

Evelyn's face flushed a deep red, then slowly returned to normal. Although they couldn't see her eyes, Alex was positive fire was leaping out of them. In the background, Georgia called a break, and the bar was suddenly quiet. Quiet enough for everyone to hear Evelyn's response.

"Get. Out."

"Evelyn, be reasonable," he pleaded. "Can't we talk about this?"

"You've done enough talking for a lifetime. Get out of my 'dump,' as you so graciously called my home," she pointed to the door. It opened and the handsome boat captain walked in and looked at the two.

"Everything okay here?" he asked Evelyn.

"No," she said.

"Yes," Nick said, simultaneously. "This is our business, Juke; go away."

Juke searched Evelyn's face. "I'll be right over here."

Evelyn rolled her eyes. "Juke, I'm fine."

Nick smirked. "Give it up. She hasn't been yours to defend for a very long time."

Juke rolled his shoulders back, but Evelyn put a hand on his arm. "I'm fine," she repeated. "Really. But thank you." She waited until he acknowledged her and then removed her hand. He stepped a few feet away to give her room and Evelyn turned back to her now ex-fiancé. The entire bar watched, rapt. "I made a mistake listening to you and giving control of my home to that monster. I won't make the mistake of marrying you. Leave."

Nick's face twisted with rage and he grabbed Evelyn's shoulders. "No, Evelyn, you don't understand. I did all of it for you!" He tried steering her out the door. "Please, come with me. Let's talk about this. I can't live without you."

"He's the Village President?" William muttered to Alex, who shushed him.

Evelyn struggled against Nick's grip. Juke jumped up from his seat, and Alex could hear a commotion behind her. Before Juke could reach the couple, Evelyn slapped Nick with a force that bent his head back. "Don't you EVER touch me again."

"You do and I'll kill you," Juke said.

Evelyn whipped her head to glare at her erstwhile defender. "I said I've got this," she hissed.

"Not if I get to him first," said Georgia, who was now standing, arms crossed, three feet away from the trio with her band behind her. "Or me," they each chorused.

Nick rubbed his cheek and glared at the faces staring at him with anger. "Small towns. What a bunch of backwards hicks. You'll all be gone soon. Kaine's going to turn this rinky-dink backwater into a place people actually want to visit, and there'll be no room for any of you." He stormed out. The room collectively exhaled.

Evelyn slumped. Juke reached out, but she stopped him. "Thanks, but I'm fine." She gave a small smile to everyone watching her. "Really, I am." Her eyes dropped to her feet and then Evelyn lifted them and gazed around the room. "Thank you, all, for having my back. Brenda?" She called to the bartender. "I think we all need a drink."

"And put it on Nick's tab!" Georgia shouted. Everyone applauded.

Evelyn returned to her barstool next to Alex. "Well, that was exciting. Probably not what you expected…"

William smiled at her. "We're always up for a little excitement."

"But I'm sure it's not *that* kind of excitement," Evelyn replied. "I'm glad you two are the only writers or tourists here tonight. Everyone else is local." Her eyes drifted to a woman sitting by herself in the corner. "Except her."

Alex turned. She made eye contact with Deborah, who stared at her over the rim of her martini glass and kept staring while she set the drink down, plucked an olive from a spear, and bit into it. Alex shivered. *Wonder why she's here, and without Kaine*, she thought, then tore her eyes away. "Big crowd for a Monday night," she remarked to Evelyn.

"Always is when Georgia's playing."

"Thanks, hon." The three turned around to face Georgia, who had moved to the bar and stood next to Evelyn. The older woman stared at Alex. Her brows furrowed and then relaxed. "I know you—you're Alex Paige."

Alex smiled. "You remember me."

"Course I do. Is Kaine why you're here?"

"No. I'm a travel writer now. Sue Morris invited William and me, along with a few other journalists." Alex paused. "Seeing Kaine was the last thing I expected."

"Ah. Getting a bit more than Sue bargained for, eh?" Georgia caught the bartender's eye, gave her a slight nod, and then searched Alex's face. "He's doing it again, you know."

"So I gathered. Back destroying lives for his almighty dollar. It's all a stupid game to him." Alex fumed. "I knew he'd been out of prison for a while, but I can't believe he'd have enough money to invest in a place like this."

William leaned in. "People like Kaine always get money."

Georgia tilted her head and squinted her eyes a bit. "Maybe it's a good thing you're here." She nodded. "Yep. Definitely a good thing." She grabbed the drink Brenda had placed on the bar and turned without a word, heading back to the stage.

William grinned at Alex. "I know that look."

"What look is that?" Evelyn asked.

"It's Alex's determined look. She gets it when she smells a good story. I've seen it a few times. First trip we were on together, as a matter of fact," he said. "She got her man then, and she'll get her man now."

"If I remember correctly, you got the man on that trip," Alex ribbed.

"Ha! That's right. I wonder whatever happened to him?" William leaned back, narrowed his eyes at Alex, and crossed his arms over his chest. "Yep. You're in. Evelyn?" he said and then tipped his head towards his friend. "Alex is on the case. I bet she'll dig something up about this whole deal. Maybe she can help save the Mast."

A hint of hope lit up Evelyn's eyes. "What do you need?"

"All the paperwork you've got." Evelyn started to get up and Alex stopped her. "Later. For now, though, I need a few minutes of Georgia and her band. And I think if you don't go talk to that tall hunk of gorgeous, he's going to come barreling over here any minute."

"And if you don't go talk to him, I will." William piped.

Evelyn turned slightly, just enough to see Juke. A small smile curved her lips and she visibly relaxed. "Yes, I should go thank him, even if I'm not exactly the frail little flower he likes to think I am." She put her hand on Alex's shoulder. "Thank you for listening."

She stood up. Before crossing the few feet to where Juke sat, she turned back to Alex. "Will you be here for a bit?"

Alex looked at her watch. It was only eight thirty, but they had an early morning. "Probably about an hour."

"That should be enough time for me to get copies of the paperwork and get it to you tonight." Evelyn paused. "But know that I don't expect anything. I may not have made my peace with this, but knowing that I've done everything possible, including accepting any help I can get, might make it easier." She strode to the table and they watched Juke stand up to pull a chair out for her.

"This is going to be fun," William said.

"What?" Alex asked.

"Watching you ferret out Kaine's dirty work. Because you know there's something dirty about all this, and you won't let him get away with it."

"No," she said. "No, I will not."

Chapter 6

It was still dark when Alex woke up. Good, she thought, she hadn't missed it. She brewed a cup of cherry cream coffee and threw on a pair of leggings, a t-shirt, and sandals. By the time she stepped outside, the sky had changed to a dusty periwinkle. She slipped off her shoes so she could feel the cool, damp grass with her toes. Dew darkened the top of the sand, creating an optical illusion that made the beach look like a mini-Sahara. She walked to where it was hard-packed from the water going in and out and let the gentle waves kiss her toes. The water was so calm, the lake barely shimmered with the reflection of the rising sun. Stripes of fuchsia and orange spread across the horizon, and she felt the world awaken.

This was her time, this early morning, this time of quiet. It's when she felt most at peace, when everything seemed possible. Alex sat in a blue Adirondack chair and pulled her knees up to her chin. She imagined what it would be like to live there, in that spot, and know that her family had made it possible. Although she and

William had smirked at Sue's "peninsular paradise" the night before, there'd been no malice; no sarcasm. Alex agreed with her. This was a piece of paradise, a place where a person could relax, live, enjoy every moment.

She felt a sense of calm wash over her. Calm, underlaid with determination. She blew the steam off the top of her coffee, took a sip, and thought about what she'd read so far from Evelyn's paperwork. When she'd gotten back to the room the night before, she'd found a three-inch-thick file sitting on the desk. Typical Kaine. Bury them in minutiae. Last night she'd given the file a quick once-over, marking a few places she wanted to investigate further. By getting up to watch the sunrise, she'd also given herself about an hour to read more thoroughly before she'd have to meet everyone. It wouldn't be enough to go over all of it, but it was a start.

Frankly, Alex was surprised that the trip was continuing as planned. Then again, she and William were the only writers who were privy to what had happened with Evelyn and Nick, and she didn't think any of the others knew of Kaine's history. On the surface, he just seemed like a slick willy who was full of himself and his shiny suits. He'd certainly fooled Harriet, but that was no surprise. She always had been about style over substance.

Alex shook her head to clear those thoughts from her mind. The drama would embroil her soon enough. For now, she wanted to embrace the peace of early morning solitude.

Someone else had the same idea, she noticed. She saw Evelyn standing on the docks, arms crossed over her chest, gazing at the horizon. Evelyn turned her head, and they acknowledged each other with slight nods. Alex heard a crack in the distance. The two women sharply looked across the marina. It seemed to come from the reserve. The sound didn't repeat. Probably nothing, Alex thought, and she swung her feet to the grass, strapped on her sandals, and walked to her room. She had enough time to shower and read through a few more of Kaine's documents before meeting Sue and the rest. It would be a full day of exploration, but with her morning ritual, the fears of the afternoon before—could she do this? would she remember how?—dissipated with the rising sun like dew.

"Good morning, everyone," Sue smiled at the writers gathered around her in the lobby. "Looks like we're still waiting for Harriet—"

"I'm here," she huffed. "My alarm clock didn't work."

"No problem. We're only five minutes behind schedule. However, Mr. Kaine is a stickler for punctuality, so we better get going."

The group of writers piled into two golf carts, one driven by Sue and the other by Lars. He paced back and forth as Sue talked and then sat in the front golf cart, his leg bouncing. Alex took a seat next to the tourism director in the other cart. Sue was a professional and tried to keep her feelings hidden, but Alex had a hunch she wasn't too pleased with the change of plans Kaine had announced so abruptly the night before. "I'm surprised to see Lars here instead of Evelyn," Alex said after a few minutes, hoping to start a conversation.

"He wouldn't miss it for the world," Sue said while turning the cart onto the road leading to the Reserve. "Excuse me for a moment." She stopped and got out to pick up a sign objecting to the golf course. When she got back to the cart, she slipped it into the gap between the front seats and the rear facing back seats. Alex noticed it had fresh tire tracks on it. "Lars is obsessed with Kaine's plans for a golf course," Sue continued, and Alex noted the dropped "Mr."

"How's the community feel about it?"

Sue's lips compressed as she considered her answer. "There are those who think it will be a great boon to Alvin's Landing and Door County."

"And the rest?"

"People here are passionate about their home," Sue deflected. "And here we are! Hello, Mr. Kaine, Deborah." She looked around. "Isn't Nick supposed to be here?"

"Yes, he is," Kaine barked, then glared at Deborah. "Find out where he is."

"Yes, Mr. Kaine." The assistant pulled her phone out of her oversized Louis Vuitton bag, walking away a few paces as she placed the call.

Kaine sat on the back of the golf cart facing the group, mounting it like a throne. The tires sunk under his weight. A few raindrops fell, and he frowned at the sky. Deborah ran over, grabbed an enormous umbrella from the front of the cart, and unfurled it over Kaine's head. "It went straight to voicemail," she said. "I don't know what could have happened to him."

"Nevermind," said Kaine. "We'll start without him." He instructed the group to get into their carts and follow him. Deborah drove, swerving slowly around potholes and rough patches where asphalt used to be. Their first stop overlooked Lake Michigan. The wind picked up and waves rolled in, causing water to spew out of a blowhole.

"This whole peninsula is limestone," Sue explained. "The lake carves out caves, and when the water's calm you can kayak into them. It's one of my favorite things to do in—"

"Now this will be one heck of a water hazard," Kaine interrupted, like he hadn't even realized someone else had been talking. "Can't you see it? This place is just screaming for a golf course." He gestured towards the dunes a little further up the shore. "I mean, Mother Nature's already provided sand traps, am I right?"

"Isn't this area protected?" William asked. "I thought it was a nature reserve."

"Oh, sure, it is, but even the tree huggers can see a good deal when it's dropped in their laps." Kaine turned to Deborah. "Call Nick again," he said, then spoke to the group. "I want him to get the credit, because he set it all up. And in about—" he looked at his watch, "two hours, it'll be official."

Alex breathed in the damp air that smelled of pine and wanted to scream. She could see what Kaine envisioned: the forest of evergreens replaced by chemically treated grass. The dunes no longer home to nesting birds and instead shaped into a playground for man. The bottom of the lake littered with balls.

"What do you mean by 'official'?" Alex asked.

"At ten this morning, the County Board Chairman's going to sign the order giving us this land to develop into the best golf course in the country. He and Nick go way back," he chuckled. "It really is who you know."

The man had no shame. He'd learned nothing from his time in prison, and Alex knew he never would. She wondered how Evelyn could have ended up engaged to someone who would be involved in a scheme like this, but then she remembered her own blindness to Ben's faults and knew she shouldn't judge.

They got back into the carts and resumed following Deborah and Kaine. For the next hour, he stopped every few hundred yards to tell them what hole was going where. Each one replaced something irreplaceable. The peninsula had little old growth because of excessive logging in the late 1800s and early 1900s, but it had rebounded with fervor. Century-old trees towered, and the ecosystem was unique. But greed, always greed, meant people like Kaine wanted to defile this escarpment and any other place they thought could bring in a profit.

It shouldn't have been possible, but Alex knew the same thing had happened further down Wisconsin's coast. Despite passionate pleas and protracted court filings, developers had converted protected dunes into a golf course based on their assurance that they would preserve other areas instead. Land, however, is not easily exchanged for other land.

The group pulled into a small parking lot next to a wooden overlook, maneuvering around an older Subaru Outback and a Tesla, which was parked across two of the four spaces. Caution tape draped at the base of the structure whipped in the increasing wind.

Kaine saw them looking dubiously at the structure. "Pay no attention to that," he said, gesturing to the yellow ribbon.

"Mr. Kaine," Sue objected. "I'm not sure this is a good idea."

He brushed off her concerns. "I've been assured this overlook is perfectly safe. They're just CYA because some nails are rusty. It'll be coming down anyway."

The writers and Lars huddled as Sue pulled out a bag stuffed in the front of her cart and extracted plastic ponchos, distributing them around the group. Kaine and Deborah declined. The personal assistant scurried out of the cart to once again shelter her boss with the massive umbrella, then checked her phone. "We're right on time. Still no word from Nick."

Kaine glanced at his watch again and motioned for the writers to climb. "We'll make this fast. I want you to see where the spa will be."

As far as overlooks go, this one was fairly short at only three stories tall, with landings every half-story. They began climbing back and forth as the stairs zig-zagged. Harriet stopped at the second landing to catch her breath. Alex maneuvered around her, followed closely by William. Wind pulled at her poncho and she grabbed the sheer plastic hood to pull it back over her head. The rain picked up, slashing diagonally. The wooden beams creaked and the overlook swayed. *Safe my butt*, Alex thought. *This is just like one of his buildings.*

She wanted to get this over with and sped up, pulling ahead of the group and widening the gap until she was a flight above the others. Then she rounded the last landing and climbed the final few steps. And stopped.

Alex saw the shoes first. Then the pants, shirt, face, hair, plastered wet against his scalp. An arm, flung over his head. A gun. Then Evelyn came into focus. Kneeling. Keening. Crying silently over her ex-fiancé.

Chapter 7

Evelyn turned to Alex, her eyes haunted. She moaned, rocking back and forth. Alex rushed over and footsteps clambered up the stairs behind her. She gripped Evelyn's shoulders, helped her stand up, and guided her to the bench that lined the railings. She pulled out her water bottle and started to give it to Evelyn when she noticed the blood on the other woman's hands. Reacting on instinct, she quickly took off her poncho and draped it over Evelyn before sitting next to her. William reached the top and Alex tipped her head towards Nick. He covered the dead man with his poncho.

"Quick thinking," he said, and sat down on Evelyn's other side.

"It's not my first murder scene," she murmured. "I can't tell you how much I hated that beat."

Harriet breached the top of the stairs. Her eyes rounded and she screamed. Behind her, Heather and Greg stopped and stared before running to opposite sides and vomiting over the railings. Jackie froze. William searched Alex's eyes over the top of Evelyn's head. "What happened?" he asked, then quickly recovered. "Sorry. Of course you don't know. How could you know?" It was, understandably, the most flustered Alex had ever seen him. He turned to Evelyn. "Are you okay?" He huffed and rolled his eyes at himself. "Of course you're not okay," he said.

Evelyn stared through the plastic poncho at the blood drying to a rusty brown on her hands, the same rusty brown that coated the nails in the overlook's struts. She looked up at Alex, her eyes haunted. "Juke."

Alex understood. "Where's your phone?" she asked.

"Pocket," she mumbled. "Back pocket."

"Can you stand for a moment? I'll reach in and get it." All three knew they couldn't wash the blood off of Evelyn's hands, as awful as it was to let it dry and cake, embedded in every crevice. Alex pulled the phone out and found Juke's number. She made eye contact with William and he nodded, understanding that he needed to stay with Evelyn while she called. She crossed to the other corner of the overlook. Past the body. Past Nick's body. It may not have been her first murder scene, but this was the first time she knew the victim.

Juke answered. "Evie? What's up?"

"Juke, this is Alex Paige."

"Who?"

"I'm one of the writers. It's not important. Listen, I need you to get to the overlook at the Reserve right away. I don't know if there are others; it's the one that's been closed off."

"Why? What's going on? Where's Evie?" His concern was palpable.

Alex took a deep breath and focused on Lake Michigan. The wind picked up; the rain felt like spray from the rolling waves and she covered the phone with her other hand to keep it dry. "Nick is dead."

"What?!"

"Look. Just get here now, okay? I need to get back to her."

"Five."

He hung up and Alex wondered how in the world he'd make it there in five minutes, but she believed him. She wiped the phone with the hem of her shirt, which was so wet it smeared the screen instead of drying it, then gave up and put it in her back pocket. She turned and saw that Sue, Kaine, and Deborah had joined the crowd on the deck of the overlook.

Heather, Jackie, and Greg, looking stunned, moved closer to the side of the overlook nearest the cliff face. There was no bench on that side, and they were about to lean against the railing. "Stop!" Sue shouted. "Stay away from there. That side's loose." She looked around. "It's supposed to be marked off. That's why this whole thing is supposed to be marked off."

Alex bent down and saw a sliver of light where the top railing should have been flush with the post. No wonder they'd strung caution tape.

Deborah stood at the top of the stairs, staring into the woods dispassionately. Alex wasn't sure the woman had any emotions at all, which she supposed made her the perfect personal assistant, or whatever she was, for Kaine. William slumped with his elbows on his knees, and Alex returned to the bench and squeezed in between him and Evelyn.

Kaine glared at the body. "So that's where Nick's been. Crap." He shifted his eyes to Deborah. "We better get going and make sure they still sign that order."

"I should probably stay here," Deborah said. Kaine scowled, and she responded quickly. "Everything should be set—"

"Should be doesn't cut it."

She turned her head to him to speak furtively, but with the wind she spoke loud enough that Alex could hear her. "One of us needs to be here," she said. "Don't worry. I've got your alibi."

"Alibi!" he roared. "Why would I need an alibi? Look at her—she's literally red-handed." Kaine turned towards the stairs and then whipped back to the group. "Deborah will call the police -"

"Already done," Sue said, returning her phone to her pocket.

"Fine. I'm leaving. Can't get this godforsaken deal done fast enough. If this messes things up, I'll—" he laughed. "Well, guess I can't kill him if he's already dead."

He barrelled down the rickety stairs and Juke swept past him, knocking him to the side as he raced to the top. Kaine growled, but kept going. Alex noticed he'd taken the umbrella with him, leaving Deborah in what was now a deluge. The assistant didn't seem to care, merely pulled another, smaller umbrella out of her bag.

"Juke," Evelyn said, standing up. He raced to her and wrapped her in his arms, and she started sobbing. When she calmed down, he pulled back and took her face in his hands. He brought her back to the bench. Alex motioned for Evelyn to wait, and she returned the woman's phone to her back pocket before they sat.

"Evie, what happened?" Juke asked.

"I don't know."

"Isn't it obvious?" Harriet asked stridently, and they all looked at her.

"Harriet, for once, would you shut up?" Alex hissed.

Harriet puffed up, affronted. "Even you can see she killed him."

William pointed to the gun sitting a few inches from Nick's right hand. "It kind of looks like suicide."

Evelyn's head jerked up. "No, no, no," she said. "Nick would never commit suicide. He loved himself too much." She covered her mouth and froze, staring in horror. "What is wrong with me? I didn't mean that. I just meant, I mean, Nick would never..."

Sue raised her hand to stop her. "The police will be here soon. Let's let them handle it."

"I didn't kill him," Evelyn said, her voice haunted. "He texted me, asked to meet me here."

"After last night, why would you?" Juke asked.

"This is where he proposed," she whispered. "I—I figured I owed it to him."

"Owed what to him? Murder?"

"Harriet!" Sue shouted, surprising all of them. "That is enough." They all heard a siren in the distance, getting closer. "Evelyn, don't say anything else. Lars, call your lawyer."

"He's not that kind of lawyer," he objected.

"I. don't. care. Call him NOW." Lars glared at her, but did as she asked.

"Sue is right," Juke said. "Don't say anything more. Billy knows you, and he'll know you didn't do this, but it's better to be quiet." His deep voice resonated, seeming to echo the strength of the surrounding woods.

The wailing siren stopped. A door slammed. The tower rattled as the officer climbed, and Alex wondered if it could withstand the weight of so many people at once. A man in uniform, mid-height and sporting a slight paunch and a mustache that channeled Tom Selleck, reached the top of the stairs. He quickly took in the scene and Alex watched his Adam's apple shift as he swallowed. "Sue, fill me in," he requested, his voice cracking. Alex had a feeling it was the poor man's first dead body.

Sue gave him a quick sketch. He nodded throughout her summary. "Okay. Detective Pierce will be here soon. I'll need to get statements from all of you, but we'll get you out of this rain." He keyed in on Evelyn. "Detective Pierce is going to want to talk to you."

"She didn't do this, Matt."

The officer stared at Juke without comment, just talked into the radio on his shoulder, instructing someone to call the Medical Examiner in Sturgeon Bay. "Bring a canopy. Oh, and make sure the photographer comes, too." He squinted into the increasing downpour. "Whose poncho is that?" he asked.

William tentatively raised his hand.

"Thanks for that."

"It was her idea," William said, gesturing to Alex.

"I used to cover the crime beat in Chicago," she explained, while putting her hand over her eyes to shield them from the rain. The officer nodded.

Sue scrounged in her bag. "I'm sorry, you two. I could have sworn I had at least one more poncho in here."

Officer Matt spoke to Juke. "Your building's closest. We'll need to use it to get these people out of the rain."

"I'm not leaving Evie. Here." He threw his keys to Sue, who deftly caught them. "You know which one it is."

Matt turned to the tourism director and gave her strict instructions, informing her he'd escort the group to Juke's office, but everyone would have to wait until Detective Pierce arrived. Poor Sue, Alex thought, as she took in everyone sitting in the rain and avoiding the corpse in front of them. What a nightmare.

Deborah sat cross-legged across from Evelyn and Juke. Lars fidgeted in the corner nearest the stairs, glancing like a bird at everyone, everyone except Nick. There was just enough distance between Lars and Deborah that there was no room for Jackie, Heather, and Greg to sit. The three huddled as far from the body as possible without being too near the railing. Alex considered the assistant, acknowledging again that she felt an instinctual dislike for her. It was uncharacteristic; Alex genuinely liked people and had issues with very few. As the other woman pulled a compact out of her bag to examine her make-up, recognition kicked in. It's her! She looked completely different, but underneath the blonde waves, enhanced figure, and carefully applied makeup was the woman who'd sat day after day in the courtroom during Kaine's trial. She was the nondescript gatekeeper who guarded the developer's office and meekly, but consistently, refused access. This was Debbie, the same Debbie who'd been Kaine's lapdog for years.

Debbie. Now Deborah.

She couldn't believe it had taken this long for her to make the connection. Stupid chemo brain, she lamented. She wondered if her memory would ever fully return.

The other writers, except William, were on their phones. Alex caught snippets of their conversations, and from what she overheard, it was obvious they'd be heading home as soon as the police released them. Alex couldn't blame them, but she wasn't going anywhere. She rested her head on William's shoulder. "I suppose you'll be leaving as soon as you can."

"Seriously?" he exclaimed. "It's like you don't even know me. Because I know you, and I know you're sticking around, and that means so am I."

"What did I ever do to deserve a friend like you?" she asked quietly.

Another car pulled up, and the tower shook as a man climbed. When he reached the top, William inhaled. "Oh, my." With thick chestnut hair and shoulders that filled every bit of his drenched polo, the man who reached the top was exactly William's type.

"Simmer down," Alex warned. "Although good thing he just now arrived, or I'd think you were staying because of him."

"Yeah, well, you may be on your own now, Miss Marple."

The detective spoke to the officer. "Matt, I'll stay here until the Medical Examiner arrives. Take this group, except Evelyn, to Juke's and get their statements. Got it?"

"Sure thing." Matt took the keys from Sue and jangled them. "I figured that's what you'd want." He motioned for them to start down the stairs.

"Excuse me," Deborah interrupted. "Can we get this over with here? I need to meet Mr. Kaine."

"No, you don't," Detective Pierce replied. "You need to go with the rest of the group. Where is he, by the way?"

"He had an important meeting with the County Board," Deborah clipped.

"More important than murder?" Detective Pierce asked incredulously. "Of course he'd think it is. Fine. When he deigns to grace us with his presence, I'll make sure he's properly questioned."

"That won't be necessary. I have his alibi."

"I'll tell you what's necessary. Now go with Officer Hampton." He paused and pointedly looked at each of them. "All of you."

Chapter 8

Officer Matt unlocked the door, letting the group file into Juke's building. The front was a small room with a row of white plastic lawn chairs placed along windows that fronted the marina. Brochures detailing Juke's services littered the counter alongside a stack of magazines with his face on the cover. Apparently, the glossy had featured him in a piece about his boat tours a few years before. A sign on the wall behind the counter welcomed them to Brannigan's Charters. Alex recognized the name. "Sue," she said, "Is Juke related to Georgia?"

Sue collapsed into a chair. "Yes. He's her grandson."

It clicked into place. Juke was the grandson who had a job for Georgia "back home." She thought of Evelyn's comments the night before about what a small world they lived in.

On the opposite side of the room, the other writers talked into their respective phones, resuming the calls the detective had interrupted when he arrived at the tower. "I don't know." "I'll let you know when I can."

"Can't imagine it'll take too long. It's pretty cut and dried." "I'm not that kind of writer." "Maybe; we saw some of the Reserve." "Get me out of here."

That last snippet was Harriet. She'd been complaining about the "stench" from the fishing shack next door. Alex turned to face the marina and the flags whipping in the blustery wind. She looked out the side window to the parking lot and straightened as she saw Juke get out of an ancient Bronco and approach the building. Detective Pierce pulled up in an obviously unmarked police car, Evelyn looking out the window from the back seat. Her eyes followed Juke, then turned the other way.

The bell over the door rattled. "Matt, Billy wants to see you," Juke said. The officer stepped outside and walked to the car.

"How's she doing?" Sue asked gently.

"How do you expect? Scared. Confused. Sad, although why she'd be sad about that piece of work—"

"Juke. They were engaged."

"Not anymore."

"She just broke it off last night. She called me when she got home. It was obvious how furious she was with him."

"So she's got motive," Harriet muttered. Sue and Juke ignored her.

"She had every right to be. At least she's keeping quiet. Didn't say a word to Billy." Juke paused. "He's taking her to the station for questioning."

"That makes no sense!" Sue cried. "He knows she wouldn't have - couldn't have - done this. Lars, did you talk to your attorney?"

"Yeah," he said sullenly. "Don't know what good it'll do. Like I told you, he's not that kind of lawyer. But he said he'd meet her at the station."

Juke shook his head. "This inn is everything to her. I've never seen her so mad. I've certainly never seen her hit someone."

"She did what?" Harriet shrieked from across the room. "Well, there you go. Motive and obviously capable of violence. Can we go now?" she asked Officer Matt as he opened the door and walked in.

The officer clapped his hand over the jingling bells and pulled a pad of paper out of his shirt pocket. "I need everyone's statements," he said, ignoring her question. "Juke, I'm going to use your office." Juke acknowledged the officer and Matt called them, one by one, behind the counter into a room cluttered with filing cabinets and a squat desk scarred with use.

After Alex gave her statement, which, like everyone else's, was brief, she turned to Juke. "I'd like to talk with you later, if that's okay."

He grabbed a card from the counter. "That'll ring my cell. Since your tour's off this afternoon, I'll be at the station until we can get Evie out of there," he said, scowling at Matt.

Alex walked outside and the shack's scent assaulted her. It smelled of fish, yes, but it also smelled of generations of hard work, of people connected to a place. It was family and hearth and home. Evelyn's home. Juke's home. And Sue's home, too. It was worth protecting, and Alex again felt the devastation of Kaine's greed. She knew why she disliked Deborah, why she'd always disliked her, back to when she first encountered her as Debbie. It's because, like a leach, she stuck to and stuck by an unscrupulous criminal.

If Kaine had his way, the boat and fishing businesses would be gone soon, just like those Gold Coast brownstones he'd demolished. Alex considered that, with Juke's both obvious affection for Evelyn and the threat of losing his business, he had motive, too. Although why would he wait to kill Nick until after Evelyn and Lars had signed the paperwork? And if that were the reason, wouldn't Kaine have been a more suitable victim? It made little sense.

Alex turned at the tinkling of bells and waited while William walked towards her. The two followed the sidewalk around the marina towards the lodge.

"Do you think she did it?" he asked. Despite trying to sound indifferent, Alex knew this wasn't a casual question.

"No, I don't. I know I just met her yesterday, but I don't see it."

William shook his head. "I'm with you. I've never met a murderer before, but she doesn't seem the type."

"I have, and it never seemed to me that there was any discernible type. Too many variables."

"What are you going to do?"

"First thing is put on some dry clothes, then I'm going to finish going through that paperwork Evelyn dropped off. Want to help? You might see something I don't."

William groaned. "For you, yes, but only for you." His eyes roamed the approaching lodge. "And for Evelyn, too, I suppose."

They entered the inn and for the second time in two days, Alex stopped so abruptly that William ran into her. "Damn," she said.

"What? Oh. Damn is right."

A lithe man sitting with crossed legs and arms spread on the back of a couch sprang up, grinning as he approached. She stood stock still. "Hello, Alex," he purred and kissed her on the cheek. "You look fantastic."

"Ben," she stammered, "what are you doing here?"

"I heard about Kaine's little investment up here and finagled an assignment. He's always good for a feature with lots of ink," Ben said, then brazenly looked Alex's soaking wet figure up and down. "It didn't hurt to know that you'd be here."

"Stalker," William said under his breath while Alex crossed her arms over her chest. Ben's assessment of her figure reminded her- not that she could ever forget- that after the lumpectomy, she was uneven.

She flushed, angered, embarrassed, and angry that she was embarrassed. With effort, Alex unwrapped her arms, put her hands on her hips, and focused on his smirk, remembering the years of tiny belittling comments that had added up to a drastic change in her personality. She'd spent the last few months not only healing from cancer treatment but also undoing the emotional damage the man in front of her had caused.

She wasn't about to let him get to her again. Any more than he already had.

"Good luck on your assignment," she said, then walked around him and headed towards the staircase. William joined her, silent.

"I'll ring you later," Ben called after her like she was expecting him, wanting him to call.

"Don't," she said, without turning around. "I won't answer." She heard him laugh softly.

As they walked towards their rooms, William kept his silence. It was one of the things she loved about him, that he knew when not talking would help more than any attempt to provide solace or offer commiseration. They stopped at his room. He spread his arms wide and water dripped from his sleeves. "I'm going to wring myself out," William said ruefully. "But then you know what I need? I need ice cream."

"And cheese curds," she replied.

"I distinctly remember seeing something in our itinerary about a place that serves sundaes as big as your head. Our official schedule may be canceled, but I don't see why we couldn't continue on our own," William suggested.

"Agreed. I'll see you in ten." She entered her room and after a quick shower, threw on a dry sundress and grabbed the thick file from the coffee table, stuffing it and a couple notebooks into a bag.

"Shall I drive?" Alex asked when she answered his knock. They took the stairs next to her room down to the back exit to avoid any chance encounter with Ben.

"Yes, please. Bessie needs a break for a few days, and so do I."

They crossed the narrow peninsula to the Green Bay side, driving two-lane roads through forests and past cherry orchards.

"So, Ben..." William prompted.

Alex felt her heart rate increase at the realization that her ex had followed her there. The way he looked at her and the touch of his lips on her cheek made her want to scour her entire body. How could she have ever found him attractive? Why had she wasted so much time with him? Done. It was done, and she'd moved on and she would not give him any more of her energy.

"Who?" she asked slyly. "We're just going to forget him, okay?"

"Suuuure. If you think that's possible."

"We've got bigger things to focus on right now."

"Definitely," he agreed. "But I have to ask; how did he know you'd be here?"

"Because I was an idiot and checked in on social when I arrived. Just had to announce my grand return to travel writing at The Mast at Alvin's Landing."

"That's kind of your job, though."

"I know, but since I broke up with him, he's texted almost daily. Plus, he's still sending those darn flowers every week. I just ignore him and donate the flowers to a nursing home. I even blocked him, but he must have found a way to see my profiles."

William shuddered. "My dear Alex, he's totally stalking you. I can go all Terminator on him if you'd like."

Alex burst out laughing. "You'd squash him like a bug! No, that's fine. Seriously. I beat cancer. I can deal with him."

William turned and considered her. "You do feel a bit invincible now, don't you?"

She thought for a minute as she negotiated a sharp turn. "Yes and no. It's hard to explain. There are so many conflicting emotions. Gratitude that I caught it when I did, anger that I had something to catch at all, relief that it's gone, and fear that it'll return. And I feel them all at once, you know? It's not like the stages of grief. They're all there, all the time."

They'd reached a town filled with white buildings and Alex pulled into a spot in a public parking lot next to the bay. She turned off the car and turned to William. "The biggest thing I struggle with is feeling helpless, like it's all out of my control."

"Is that why you want to help Evelyn?"

"That's a big part of it, yes. It's something I can do."

"Do you have any idea who might have killed Nick?"

"I have ideas. It seems like he wasn't the most popular guy. Not Kaine-level unpopular, but nobody except Evelyn has seemed particularly upset that he's dead."

"True," William said, and tipped his head towards red and white striped awnings. "Time for ice cream."

Chapter 9

The restaurant was nearly full; a hostess seated them in the last available red vinyl booth. Their server greeted them, introducing herself as Joy. She was a lean woman with corded arms who looked like she'd spent decades outdoors. They ordered cheese curds and two root beers, and each chose a small sundae for dessert. William settled in and Alex noticed a television in the corner. A talk show ran in the background. As Joy returned with their basket of fried cheese and a couple of frosty mugs, the screen switched to a news desk. William turned to see what Alex and Joy were looking at. A caption scrolled:

Breaking News: Village President Nicholas Langley was found dead this morning at the Alvin's Landing Nature Reserve.

"Couldn't have happened to a nicer man," Joy said.

Alex looked at her curiously. "You don't seem surprised."

"Do you know Nick?" she asked, and the two nodded.

"We met him yesterday," William explained. "And had the misfortune of seeing him this morning." William grabbed a cheese curd, blew on it, then shook his fingers. "Oof, those are hot!" he exclaimed.

Alex rolled her eyes at him. "You do that every time fried food hits the table."

"What can I say? I don't like to wait," he said with a wink.

Joy looked up at the screen, which now showed the overlook and a dramatic shot of the caution tape, hanging forlornly and dripping rain into a shallow pool. The closed caption read: *Vote on the Nature Reserve's partial transfer to Chicago developer Trevor Kaine delayed out of respect, Board Chairman Phillip Eliot issued in a brief statement.*

"What Evelyn ever saw in him..." Joy said. "Gossip is she dumped him last night." She laughed a little. "Heard it was quite a scene. You know Evelyn?"

"Yes, we met her, too," Alex said, deciding she couldn't wait anymore and grabbed fried cheese from the basket. "I like her."

Joy's face crinkled. "She's the best. When we had that awful storm last October, power went out everywhere. They had backup generators, and she offered up rooms to anyone who needed them—and there were a lot, let me tell you. She even fed everyone, handed out all the free food you could eat. That woman built up some serious loyalty. Her only downside was Nick. Not a surprise someone finally murdered the jerk."

"It might have been suicide," William countered.

Joy laughed. "Ha! That man would never commit suicide. He loves himself too much," she said, unconsciously echoing Evelyn's earlier statement. She moved off to greet a table of new patrons.

Alex and William dipped their cheese curds into ranch dressing and sipped on their root beers. They began hearing Nick's name murmured as the news made its way around the room. They finished the fried cheese just as Joy came back with two giant towers of ice cream crowned with whipped cream. "Fess up," she said. "What'd you mean by seeing Nick this morning?"

Alex tore her eyes from their idea of a "small" sundae, but not before plucking the cherry from the top of her dessert. She motioned for William to go ahead. To his credit, he gave the briefest of explanations, but he couldn't avoid telling her that Evelyn was a suspect.

"There is no way that woman could kill anyone, no matter how much he deserved it," Joy said while picking up the empty basket where the cheese curds had been. She snapped the fingers of her empty hand. "You're a couple of the writers Sue brought in, aren't you?" They nodded. "That's how you met Nick and Evelyn. Probably met Kaine, too. You know, it's Nick's fault she had to sell to Kaine. The whole golf course was Nick's idea, and that viper leapt at it. Plenty of people are mad about that deal, and they blame Nick. At least the ink's not dry yet."

She headed towards the kitchen and Alex dug her spoon into the bowl, pulling out a heaping scoop of vanilla ice cream, bits of toffee, and hot fudge. She patted the paperwork beside her. "Let's eat what we can and head to that gazebo across the street; I want to go through this file some more."

William grunted, but he agreed.

Alex slumped against the back of the bench and set the stack of papers between herself and William with a sigh. They were sitting on the side of the gazebo that was in the sun, which had come out in full force while they'd been stuffing their faces, and it had dried the wood. The parts in the shade were still dark from the rain and pools of water collected where years of use had shaped the bench.

"That sounds like frustration," William said.

"It is. It all looks legit. Kaine must have gotten better lawyers," she complained. "The only way can cancel the sale is if he doesn't deposit the escrow amount by Thursday."

"I may have found something," he said, moving her stack of papers to his other side and scooting closer. He tapped a clause in the Exhibit she'd given him to review. "This right here. It looks like the sale of the Mast itself may be contingent upon his ability to turn the Reserve into a golf course." William's voice reeked of disgust. "At least, he can choose to cancel the contract if the county board doesn't approve the transfer."

Alex read it and gazed thoughtfully at the bay, watching a kayaker paddle slowly along the horizon. "And with the board's decision to delay the vote..."

"Unless Kaine can get them to vote tomorrow, it looks like he may not get his little playground."

"Evelyn will need her attorney to confirm that, but it could be a way to get her out of this mess. Why would he want The Mast if he can't build his course?"

"She's still going to have the same issues with losing it, won't she?" William asked.

"Maybe. Depends on why they're in such dire straits," Alex responded. She put her hand out and William handed her the Exhibit. She put those papers, as well as the stack she'd been reviewing, back in her bag. "I saw Evelyn this morning."

"Really? Before the, um, you know? Where? When?"

"At the marina. I'd gotten up early to watch the sunrise—"

William groaned. "I do not know how you do that."

She elbowed him. "It's my time, okay? Anyway, the sun had just come up, so it must have been about a quarter after six, and I saw her standing on the dock watching the sunrise as well." Alex stopped, remembering something from that morning. "Wait a minute. I wonder..."

"Wonder what?"

Alex shook her head. "It could be nothing." She pulled Evelyn's card from her notebook and dialed. "She's not answering. I'm going to call Juke and see if they've released her."

She stood up and paced back and forth in the center of the gazebo. The kayaker had disappeared, but she saw a sailboat heading out of the bay, a shallow wake behind it. Their original itinerary had them out on the water right about now, she thought, and then the boat captain picked up. "Yes?" Juke answered, his voice gruff.

"It's Alex. Is Evelyn still at the station?"

"Yes. It's ridiculous."

"Okay. We'll be there in about half an hour. If you're able to get her out, call me so I can meet you somewhere later, okay?"

"Why? Why do you care?"

"Because I know she didn't kill him."

"How could you possibly know that? You just met her. I ask again. Why do you care?"

Alex exhaled, understanding his confusion at her motives. She'd question them if she were him. There was too much at stake to trust a stranger blindly. "Because of Kaine," she started.

"What about that piece of—"

"I may not know Evelyn, but I know Kaine, and he's capable of anything." Alex rushed on before Juke could interrupt her again. "What he's planning to do here is a crime and pure greed, and I wouldn't put a single thing past him if it got him what he wants."

"Doesn't seem like it worked this time," William said, overhearing Alex's side of the conversation.

She continued. "Listen, I just want to help. I, I like Evelyn. She could take Kaine's millions and run, but she won't do that. She won't let him destroy this place." Alex paused. "Please. Let me," she glanced at William, "let us help."

She heard the noise of the police station in the background as Juke considered. "Fine. I'll call you if we leave." He hung up.

William looked at her curiously. "Why don't we wait until she's released to meet up with them? Seems like a waste to drive to Sturgeon Bay."

"Because I thought of something."

"What? You can't keep me in suspense."

Alex shook her head. "I don't want to jinx it."

Juke hadn't called by the time they pulled up to the two-story station. It wasn't large but was obviously fairly new, with a front wall of blue glass windows that reflected the afternoon sun, blinding them as they approached the sliding doors.

Inside, Juke prowled like a caged beast, never taking his eyes off the door in the corner. Kaine banged his fist on the counter. "They demanded that I give a statement, and I demand to be seen now. I'm not waiting any longer!" Alex thought the only thing missing was a bombastic *Don't they know who I am?*

Deborah placed her hand on Kaine's arm again, a familiar gesture Alex had seen her make repeatedly in the last nineteen hours. Alex noticed she had changed into another pencil skirt and another pair of stilettos. *When did she find the time?* she wondered. Kaine brushed his assistant's hand off his forearm. "Don't try to manage me. Do you know what's at stake?"

"Of course I do," she said through clenched teeth. "Do you?" He twisted his head to her. "We need their cooperation."

To their right, Ben leaned against a wall, one leg crossed over the other, with his continual smirk plastered on his face. He held his phone towards Kaine and Deborah, Ben's right elbow resting on his left hand, which was wrapped across his chest. Alex could see the base of the phone was pointing towards the room and knew Ben was recording the conversation. He blew a kiss in her direction and she resolutely turned her back on him.

Kaine rolled his head, stretching his neck from side to side, front to back. He turned back to the officer behind the counter. "If you could please," he grated, "let

Detective Pierce know that Trevor Kaine is ready to give his statement."

The officer laconically picked up the phone, dialed, and delivered the message.

In the corner, the door opened and Evelyn walked out, flanked by Detective Pierce and a short, portly man with a tonsure haircut. Juke stopped, hurried towards her. She focused on Kaine, and her eyes brimmed with contempt until she noticed Alex and William, and then turned to Juke. She seemed stronger, and Alex assumed the shock had worn off and anger filled her instead. Alex had seen this reaction in others she had known to be wrongfully accused. It was a good thing. It meant Evelyn was ready to fight.

"What is *she* doing out here?" Kaine exploded.

"Mr. Kaine," Detective Pierce clipped. "Calm down now or I'll have to detain you."

"You were there! You were all there!" Kaine blustered, gesturing at Evelyn. "You saw the blood on her hands."

"We can't hold her unless we charge her."

"Can't you hold her for 24 hours or something? And why don't you charge her? It's obvious she killed him. If we were in Chicago—"

"This isn't Chicago, Mr. Kaine."

"No, it most certainly is not."

Detective Pierce raised his hand to stop him. "I understand you're here to make a statement. Follow this officer and I'll be with you shortly." The man behind the desk motioned for Kaine to walk through the door.

"Deborah Minnow? You'll need to wait out here," Pierce said.

Deborah crossed to the row of chairs against the wall, heels clicking. She sat down and confronted Alex's gaze and then turned to her boss. "Mr. Kaine, I will contact Mr. Avalon." She looked at Detective Pierce, but her message was unmistakably for her boss. "That's his attorney, and I'm sure he'll advise Mr. Kaine to remain quiet."

Kaine followed the detective and replied, his tone biting like a Midwest winter storm. "Thank you, Deborah. I think I know how this works."

"Of course he does," Alex whispered to William. "It's not his first rodeo." William stifled a laugh.

Evelyn backed up as Kaine neared her. Juke moved to get between them, but one look from her stopped him. The door to the station burst open and Georgia rushed in.

"I did it! I killed Nick!"

Chapter 10

A hush covered the room. Ben laughed, a single bark. Juke and Evelyn yelled at the same time. "Grandma!" "Georgia!" Alex and William looked at each other, looked at Georgia, looked at Detective Pierce. "Is this what you didn't want to tell me?" William whispered.

"Not even close. What is she doing?" Alex answered.

"You don't think she did it?"

"Not on your life," she grimaced. "Bad turn of phrase. No, not for one second, just like I know Evelyn didn't do it."

Detective Pierce spoke to the officer escorting Kaine. "Get Matt and tell him to come up here now." He faced Georgia. "Ms. Brannigan-"

"Billy, I've known you since you were in diapers. I *changed* your diapers."

"Fine, then. Georgia, what are you doing?"

"I'm confessing. I killed Nick."

"Uh, huh. And I'm a rock star."

"He could be," William said under his breath. Alex smiled. The man was incorrigible.

"Grandma, what are you doing?" Juke asked, repeating Billy's question. "Are you doing this to protect Evie? She's released—see?" he said while gesturing to the redhead.

"Released doesn't mean diddly. I did it." Georgia thrust her wrists out. "Arrest me."

"Oh, for heaven's sake," Billy said to her, rolling his eyes. "I am not going to handcuff you or arrest you, yet. I will, however, question you."

"This woman threatened Mr. Langley last night," Deborah said, then looked at Juke, "and so did he. What was it he said? Oh, yes. 'I'll kill you,' I believe was the phrase."

Billy started. "Is that true?"

"He put his hands on Evie," Juke explained. "So yes, I got angry. But no, I didn't kill him. And neither did my grandmother." He scowled at the small grinning woman.

"Okay then. Georgia, come with me." Billy pointed at Juke. "I'll get to you as soon as I'm done with this one."

Georgia walked by Alex and winked. Alex dropped her head to hide the smile. Out of the corner of her eye, she could see that Ben, however, had witnessed the entire exchange.

"Georgia, I don't know what you're doing, but we're going to get you out of this," Evelyn said.

"Don't you worry. I'll be just fine." She walked through the door, and Billy turned to follow her.

"Wait, Detective Pierce?" Alex called after him and he stopped. "Can you tell me, do they know the time of death yet?"

Billy looked around the room before settling his eyes on Alex. "Yes, but I'm afraid I can't release that information."

"Fine, but if it was around 6:15, Evelyn couldn't have done it."

The detective stiffened, then composed himself. "Why would you think it happened at that time, specifically?"

Alex could feel the eyes on her. "Because I saw her this morning at the marina. We were both up watching the sunrise. Around 6:15, we heard a crack from the direction of the Reserve."

"Ah," William said, "so that's what you were alluding to."

"Why didn't you say anything, either of you?" Billy asked.

"Because I didn't know what it was. It was just a crack, and it happened once. It could have been a tree branch falling," Alex explained. "Besides, I'd forgotten about it until a little while ago. That's why we wanted to meet you here," she said to Juke.

Evelyn frowned. "It was definitely a gun shot. Can't believe I didn't think of that." She turned to Billy. "But he sent me a text message at eight asking me to meet him at the overlook. He had to still be alive then."

Deborah had stood up and was now lounging against the wall, adopting a pose eerily similar to Ben's. She investigated her nails and pushed down a wayward cuticle. "Maybe you sent the text to yourself after you killed him."

"That is monstrous!" Evelyn cried. "Who would do such a thing?"

Deborah looked up and made eye contact with Kaine. "A murderer."

"Alright, folks, that's enough," Billy said. "Georgia, come with me. Mr. Kaine, go with Officer Taylor. You three," he said to Alex, William, and Ben, "go do whatever you writers do, but don't do it here."

"Um, we're not with him," William protested, gesturing at Ben.

"Don't care. Just get out of here. And you," he said, glaring at Deborah. "I assume you'll be waiting for Mr. Kaine?"

"Yes, of course."

"Fine. I'll want to talk to you as well."

"I already gave my statement to Officer Hampton," Deborah said.

"I'm aware of that. Wait here," Billy replied.

She gave him a curt nod, then turned back to read a text on her phone. "Mr. Kaine, Mr. Avalon has replied and he will be here in an hour."

Alex walked outside, followed closely by William. The door closed behind them, so she didn't catch Kaine's reply, but she heard his derisive tone. "That woman," she said. "I've never seen someone so slavishly devoted to another human being."

"You sure Kaine's human?"

Alex laughed. "No, no, I am not."

Juke and Evelyn followed them into the late afternoon sun, the morning's storm a memory. She stopped and tilted her face up, as Alex had seen her do the day before. Like a flower, she thought. "Thank you," Evelyn said. "I think you just gave me an alibi."

"You're welcome," Alex said. "I wish I'd thought of it earlier, though."

Evelyn stopped her. "He still would have had to take me in. I touched Nick, after all." She shuddered. "What are we going to do about your grandma?" she asked Juke, jerking her head towards the station. "What was she thinking?"

"Protecting you. You know she thinks of you like her own granddaughter. That woman, I swear," he said, stuffing his hands into his jean pockets. "Billy's not going to arrest her. I hope. Look, I need to get back in there." He turned to Alex and William. "Could you give her a ride home?"

"Of course," Alex said.

Evelyn hugged Juke. "Thank you," she said, her voice muffled against his chest.

He stroked her hair gently. "For what?"

"For being there for me. Let me know when you're out, okay?"

Juke agreed, and Alex drove the three of them back to Alvin's Landing. Evelyn sat silent in the front passenger seat, watching the landscape blur past. William moved forward to speak, but Alex caught his eyes in the rearview mirror and he sat back. They needed to give her some space.

Evelyn directed them to a narrow driveway about half-a-mile south of The Mast. Her home set back from the road, sheltered by tall pines. They were the same type of pines that someone had cut long ago to build the cabin. A small garden bordered the side of the house; Alex caught glimpses of a beach and the lake.

They entered a large open space with a living room, dining area, and kitchen. Evelyn dropped her keys in a basket next to the front door, then slipped down the hall that led to the back of the house. She returned after changing into khaki shorts and a white V-neck t-shirt, her red curls pulled into a ponytail.

"Thanks for bringing me home," she said, and looked over Alex's shoulder. "Where's William?"

"He's out front. His editor called and they're trying to hash out some story ideas now that the FAM's been interrupted and he plans on sticking around."

"FAM?"

"Short for Familiarization. It's what we call these kinds of trips."

"Ah. William's freelance, isn't he?" Evelyn said as she moved into the kitchen and poured three glasses of iced tea.

Alex accepted the cool drink and sat on one of the tall bar stools at the granite-covered island. "Yes, and his relationship with his editors is everything. They know he's a pro. Always makes his deadlines, plus his photos are stunning. There's a reason he's in demand. But, he's still got to come up with new angles," she said and took a sip of her tea. She tasted some type of fruit.

"Cherry," Evelyn answered her questioning look. "You'll find that everything up here has cherries in it. So," she continued, "what about you? Don't you have an editor to answer to?"

Alex raised her glass and the ice clinked as she tipped it towards Evelyn. "Me, myself, and I," she said, while wondering if this conversation was simply a delaying tactic. She couldn't blame her if it was. A few moments of normalcy felt nice. "I'm my own publisher. After I left the paper, I started my travel website and never looked back. I do some freelance, but honestly? I make more if I publish on my site. Plus, I don't have any editors to answer to." She took another sip and smiled. "Except myself. I can be a pretty exacting boss."

"I bet," Evelyn replied. She put her glass on the counter, then placed both hands on the edge and leaned, hunching her shoulders. "I can't believe Nick was... was murdered."

"You're sure someone killed him? William seems to think it might have been suicide."

"No, it was definitely murder. Billy let it slip at the station that the angle of the wound was all wrong. It would have been impossible for him to shoot himself," Evelyn said. "But who would want to kill him?"

Alex refrained from responding with *Everyone, from what I've seen.* "Did he rub anyone the wrong way?" she asked instead.

Evelyn grunted. "Now that you put it that way... he rubbed just about everybody the wrong way. Nick tried, he really did, but he has—had—this attitude about him, like he was better than the rest of us, like he deserved more than the rest of us."

"I take it he grew up here?"

"Yep. Born and bred, as they say. He moved away shortly after I did. Juke always said he followed us to Evanston, but I told him that was ridiculous. It's not like he followed me around the country when I left Chicago."

"But he came back here once you did," Alex pointed out.

"Yes," Evelyn smiled. "He did. As soon as he learned I had cancer. He was so kind. So thoughtful. Whatever I needed. Mom was already in assisted living, and while Sue was a rock, it was nice to have Nick's help. I saw a side of him I'd never noticed before," she said wistfully. Alex wondered if she'd misread the man.

"He was a lot of things," Evelyn continued softly, "but he didn't deserve this."

Alex waited a beat. "What did you mean by 'followed us'?"

Evelyn's eyes looked down, but the corners of her mouth turned up, albeit slightly. "If anyone did the following, it was me. Juke got accepted to Northwestern, and I followed him a year later. We were high school sweethearts," she said wistfully. "And before. Seemed like we'd always be together."

"What happened? Was it Nick?"

Evelyn laughed. "No, definitely not. Not in the way you mean. I only had eyes for Juke. But Nick ended up in Evanston and he didn't quite get the hint. He was everywhere. I tried to ignore him, but it drove Juke nuts. There was one night... " she stopped.

"What?"

Evelyn sighed. "This is going to sound terrible. Juke and I were out at our regular hangout and Nick was there. He was always there. He'd sit at the bar or at a table and stare at us. It was pretty creepy, actually. I'd forgotten about that," she mused. "Anyway, one night Juke decided he'd had enough, picked Nick up, dragged him outside, and the two got in a fistfight. Or, Juke fought. Nick fell." She hesitated. "It was not Juke's finest hour."

Evelyn was right. It did sound terrible. "What happened?" Alex asked.

"Nothing. The cops came. Nick wanted to press charges, but they shrugged it off as college antics and told them to go home and sleep it off." Evelyn pulled at her earlobe. "I was pretty angry at Juke. I'd never seen him like that before. I told him I needed space. Not long after that, his dad got sick and he had to come home to take over the charter business."

"Oh."

"Yep. Oh. I stayed, graduated, and in a few years was traveling around the country managing hotels." Evelyn looked up as William came through the front door. "I was in San Diego when I heard Juke got married."

"He what?" William yelped. "Juke's married? I swear, I leave for five minutes and you learn all the juicy stuff."

Evelyn laughed. "No, not anymore. By the time I moved home, his marriage was already falling apart, but I didn't know that. Not that it would have made a difference," she said wistfully. "They divorced a few years ago." Evelyn picked up a honey crisp apple out of a bowl on the island and polished it on her t-shirt.

"So why didn't you two get back together? It's obvious there's some serious chemistry there." Alex grabbed an apple, absentmindedly mimicking Evelyn.

"Chemistry does not a relationship make." Evelyn took a bite and primly wiped a stray bit of peel from the corner of her mouth. "We'd grown so far apart... Besides, I'd already begun dating Nick."

"Those two seem like complete opposites," Alex said.

"You have no idea."

Chapter 11

Alex leaned on the counter. "On another note... I know the resort may not be your biggest concern right now, but William and I went through the contract and I think we—he—found something that might help."

Evelyn brightened. "Like I said last night, I'll take any help I can get to save the inn."

It clicked in Alex's brain that Evelyn never called The Mast a resort, although with its restaurant, live music, beach, and easy access to fishing charters, boat tours, hiking, and kayaking, it could qualify. While there wasn't an on-site spa, she'd seen from a brochure in her room that they'd partnered with a salon in Alvin's Landing so you could get in-room treatments or add a mani-pedi to your room bill. The only thing they didn't have within a few minutes was a golf course. That suited Alex just fine. She had nothing against golf or golf courses, and didn't mind swinging a club here and there, but she also knew they were environmental disasters. Besides, the peninsula already had several. It didn't need another one. It especially didn't need to destroy a unique ecosystem.

William motioned for the bag and Alex scooted it across the island. He pulled out the file and waved Evelyn over. He flipped to the section he'd flagged earlier that day. "Here," he said, pointing to the clause. "You'll want your attorney to look at this, but it looks like Kaine could cancel the sale of the Mast if the county doesn't grant his request to turn the Reserve into a golf course. Since that's such a big part of his grand plan, he may not want one without the other."

"Yes," she said, deflated. "I knew about that. But it's a done deal. The board voted this morning."

"Didn't you hear?" Alex asked. "No, you wouldn't have. You were in the police station. The board delayed the vote after hearing about Nick."

"They did?" Evelyn brightened up. "Seriously, oh, this could change everything. I'll still need to come up with the money for the taxes," she muttered, "but maybe. Maybe I can try one more time to convince the board not to approve this."

"Taxes?" Alex asked.

"Yes, that's why the sense of urgency. We're behind on our property taxes and if they're not paid, the county will seize the property, and that includes the marina and everything in it." Evelyn reached across the island for her glass and rolled it between her hands. "Nick convinced me that Kaine's 'solution' was the only way to save it, but after seeing his plans, I'd rather let the county have it."

"I have to say, I'm surprised you would have signed off on the golf course," William said, a touch of disappointment in his voice.

"I didn't. Lars did," Evelyn said bitterly. "I reviewed the contract, but Lars and our lawyer reviewed the Exhibits. Mom left The Mast to both of us, and when Lars told me the Exhibits looked fine, I signed. I should have known. Lars has never been a fan of the inn, or the Reserve, or Alvin's Landing in general."

Evelyn considered what Alex had told her. "So the board delayed the vote after learning Nick was killed..." She drummed her fingers on the countertop. "Have you heard when they've rescheduled it? It has to be before Thursday. That's when Kaine's escrow payment is due."

Alex shook her head and Evelyn pulled her phone out of her back pocket and pulled up a number. "Phil? Hi, it's Evelyn. Yes, thank you. I appreciate that. I know you two didn't always see eye to eye." She paused as the other person spoke. "Yes, well, he could be challenging. Listen, the reason I'm calling - " she laughed. "Exactly. It is? Two o'clock? Great. Thank you, Phil. I'll see you tomorrow."

"The vote's tomorrow?" Alex guessed.

"Yes. Apparently, Kaine wouldn't leave until the board told him they'd resume voting the next day. Honestly, it shocked me when I heard they were going to approve it. I know everybody on that board and three out of the five are die-hard fans of the Reserve. And all of them grew up with it. But then you've got people like my brother, who think the best thing to happen to Alvin's Landing would be to become something that's not Alvin's Landing."

Alex put the file back in her bag. "I have a question," she prompted. "You said you got a text from Nick this morning asking you to meet him?"

"Yes," Evelyn said, pulling a stray curl behind her ear. "I wasn't going to. I was still pretty angry. But that's where he proposed. It's also where he and Kaine told me about their 'offer'." She frowned. "That was Nick. All about the theatrics." Evelyn walked around to the refrigerator and refilled their iced teas.

"The police must have his phone. I wonder," Alex mused. "Since you were engaged, are you on his plan? Could you get his cell phone records?"

William winked at Alex. "I like the way you think, my dear."

"No, we hadn't commingled anything like that yet." Evelyn snapped her fingers and pointed at Alex. "But I have something better."

Alex followed her down the hall to her office, William close on her heels. They waited as Evelyn booted up her laptop. "Nick was always buying the newest phone, so he backed up everything to the cloud. He gave me access, said he wanted to show he had nothing to hide." She entered her password and opened a browser. "Not that I thought he did. So that, of course, made me wonder.

"Here it is."

Alex came around and looked over Evelyn's shoulder. The last text message was sent to Evelyn at 8:03 that morning.

Evelyn, I am so sorry. I never meant to hurt you. I don't know what I was thinking. I don't expect you to come back to me, but could you meet me at the overlook at nine? I love you.

Evelyn touched the screen. "Oh, Nick," she whispered. "I was so surprised. We both needed to be at the board meeting in Sturgeon Bay at ten, which is forty-five minutes away. Plus, I thought he'd be on the tour with you. I didn't know what to make of it."

"So that's why you met him, even after last night?" William asked.

"That was part of it. It was so out of character. I knew he'd never do anything to upset Kaine." Evelyn wiggled her bare ring finger. "I'm proof of that."

Alex pointed to the screen. "What's this?" she asked.

Tomorrow's it. Meet me at the overlook at 6:10am sharp.

Evelyn stared at the message. "It was sent last night around ten."

"Kind of early for a meeting, isn't it?"

"Not for Nick. Early bird catches the worm, you know. He was ambitious - wanted everything, and he didn't want to wait for it." Evelyn squeezed her eyes shut. "Listen to me. I slipped so easily into past-tense."

Alex shrugged. "Don't read anything into it. In a way, after last night, he *was* your past tense. Do you recognize that number?" Alex asked.

Evelyn shook her head, picked up her phone, and put it on speaker. "Let's find out."

The phone rang several times before a generic voice answered. "This number is unavailable right now. Leave a message after the tone."

Evelyn hung up. "That doesn't help." She groaned and flopped back in the chair, gazing at the ceiling. "Nick, what were you up to?" she asked, then directed her eyes back and forth between Alex and William. "I should have asked him point blank: why Kaine? Beyond the obvious answer. We could have gotten bids and put it on the market, but before anybody knew how much trouble we were in, Nick dropped this in my lap. It seemed like a gift, like the answer to all my problems. I trusted him, dammit. I trusted him."

Evelyn broke down then, sobbing, the kind of crying that wracked the body. Alex heard the pain of a woman who'd been betrayed. They let her cry, let her get it all out, or as much as she could.

After several minutes, Evelyn calmed down and Alex handed her a box of tissues she'd found on the bookshelf. Evelyn scrolled and stopped at another exchange.

I don't know if I can do this.
You have to.
It's not right.

What isn't right? Making millions? Think of what's at stake. Think of Lindsay.

Alex pointed to the name on the screen. "Lindsay checked me in. Could that be her?"

"Maybe," Evelyn considered. "She's Phil's daughter."

"The county board chair is her dad? Unless there's another Lindsay."

"There may be. We're a small community, but not that small. Still, it seems like too much of a coincidence, especially since Phil and Nick have known each other since they were kids."

Is that a threat?

You know what you need to do.

Fine. But after this, we're done.

Maybe we are. And maybe we're not.

Evelyn sat back in the chair. "What is going on? What was that all about?"

"Sounds like Nick's got something on Phil," Alex replied.

"It doesn't even sound like Nick. Not the Nick I know. Knew." Evelyn squeezed her eyes shut. "Or maybe it does. He was determined to be rich. Filthy stinking rich. Kaine-level rich."

"Or at least Kaine-on-paper rich. You know he's essentially a con artist," William said.

"What could Nick have on Phil, and what was it he wanted him to do?" Alex mused.

"I'm ninety-nine percent sure this is about the Reserve vote. That Reserve is one of Phil's favorite spots in the county. I couldn't believe it when I heard he was going to let it get ripped up for a golf course. Phil doesn't even play golf." Evelyn started to close the laptop, but Alex stopped her and took photos of the text messages on the screen.

"Nancy Drew here likes to document everything," William explained.

When she was done, Evelyn closed the computer, then pushed back her chair and stood up. "We need to go to Nick's house."

"What are you thinking?"

"If Nick does—crap," she caught herself, "did—have something on Phil, as you put it, then maybe we can find out what it is."

Evelyn grabbed her keys. Alex and William followed, and as they got into her Outback he requested they drop him off at the Mast. "Believe me, I would much rather be snooping with you two, but my editor said he needs the formal pitch for the new angle this afternoon." He fell against the back seat. "You may have the right idea with this whole being your own boss thing. Maybe I should seriously consider finally writing that book."

Alex reached around and patted William's knee. "You should. You've been talking about it for years."

"Yeah, but what a lot of work." He harrumphed and sat in silence during the short drive. Evelyn pulled up to the entrance, and William got out. He motioned for Alex to roll down her window and kissed her on the cheek. "I won't need long. You better keep me informed, Ms. Holmes."

She saluted him. "Aye-aye, Watson." She watched him enter the inn as they drove away.

Evelyn looked sideways at Alex. "You two are close."

Alex grinned. "He's the best. We've got one of those relationships where we don't talk often, but when we do it's like no time has passed. We didn't talk much in the past year with this," she gestured to her hair. For some reason, that was how she always referred to her cancer, never by indicating where it actually occurred. "Plus, he was in a lot of remote places with no connection. Honestly, I envied him, but I was happy to know he wasn't stuck at home like I was."

Alex turned her head and appraised Evelyn. "I heard you let people whose homes were damaged in the storm stay at the inn and provided meals for anyone who needed it. That's pretty amazing of you."

Evelyn blushed. "It didn't seem right to have this huge place with empty rooms when there were people with no place to stay and who couldn't get home. Plus, we've got a gigantic kitchen. We had the resources." She paused as she turned into a driveway flanked by stone columns. The asphalt wound and curved through a grove of birch trees up a slight incline. "At least, I thought we did. We'd had several full seasons before last fall. I still don't know how we got into the mess we did. We should have had enough to weather a couple of down years."

They rounded one last bend and Alex gawked at the McMansion in front of her with a pearl Lexus parked in front. "This is Nick's house?"

"Oh yes. He was so proud when he built this monstrosity, said he couldn't wait for us to be married and for me to move in." Evelyn shuddered. "Why is beyond me. For two people? I mean, can you imagine the cleaning?"

Alex agreed. "Is that his car?"

Evelyn shook her head. "No. He drives a Tesla. It was at the overlook this morning."

Evelyn pulled up behind the Lexus in the circular drive and the two women walked to the front door, which was slightly open. "Hello?" Evelyn called. "Hello? Who's here?"

A click-clack echoed down the long center hallway. A thin yet voluptuous blonde appeared, her stilettos tapping on the marble floor, her steps constrained by her tight pencil skirt.

Chapter 12

"Deborah," Evelyn exclaimed. "What are you doing here?"

"Maybe now we should call Billy," Alex said.

Deborah stopped in front of them. She put her hands on her hips, challenging Alex. "You don't like me, do you?"

"I don't know you enough to like or dislike you," Alex replied, knowing full well she was being dishonest. She absolutely did *not* like this woman, whose lips thinned as she raised an eyebrow.

"Not really an answer. That's fine. You don't have to like me. You do, however, need me."

"Why would I need you?"

"You both do. Especially you." Deborah looked pointedly at Evelyn. "To find out who killed Mr. Langley."

"Deborah, it's just the three of us here," Evelyn said. "Please drop the act. I know you've known Nick for years."

"How do you know that?" Deborah asked. Alex could hear a lift of what sounded like hope in the woman's voice. *Now that's interesting*, she thought.

"Because he's been working with Kaine for years and anybody who works with Kaine works with you. Even I can see that."

Deborah looked crestfallen for a split moment, then returned to her automaton self. "That makes sense. Yes. That makes sense."

Alex and Evelyn exchanged a glance. This woman was definitely an odd one. "Deborah, why are you here? What are you doing in Nick's house?" Evelyn asked.

"And how did you get in?" Alex added.

"I know the code."

"Why?"

"Because Mr. Kaine and I were here frequently to discuss details of the sale."

"Why have I never seen you?" Evelyn asked.

"How would you? You were never here," Deborah admonished. "Nick constantly complained that he couldn't wait for the sale of The Mast to be completed, so he might finally have some time with you."

"What did he think was going to happen? He knew I wouldn't quit working. Nevermind. It doesn't matter. What does matter is: Why are you here?"

Deborah sighed, and for the first time, Alex saw a touch of vulnerability as she moved into the front parlor and walked towards a white leather chaise lounge. The entire room was white, except for a photo of a golf green above the mantle. "May I?" Evelyn nodded, and Deborah sat down, then took off one of her stilettos and began rubbing the ball of her foot. "Thank you."

"Why do you wear those?" Alex asked. They looked like pure torture devices.

"Because it's what Mr. Kaine expects," Deborah replied, without a hint of rancor. "He's particular." She put the high heel back on her foot and sat on the edge of the lounge. She looked almost coquettish with her prim posture. "Which is why I'm here."

"Go on," Alex prompted.

"Mr. Kaine wanted me to find out everything I could about Mr. Langley's, er- Nick's, interaction with the board."

"Why?" Evelyn asked.

"Because of the abrupt decision this morning to delay the vote."

"Why wouldn't they delay it?" Alex asked. "They did it out of respect for their Village President. But of course Kaine wouldn't understand that."

Deborah glared at her. "He understands respect just fine. That delay, however, could be a problem."

"Yes, I know," Evelyn said. "Without the Reserve for his golf course, The Mast means nothing to him."

"Oh, darn," Alex said. Evelyn gave her a small smile.

"Look, I know you didn't want to sell to Mr. Kaine," Deborah said to Evelyn, "but the sale will go through, no matter what."

"No matter what? Like, for instance, murder?"

Deborah laughed, an unpleasant braying that set Alex's nerves on edge. Or, more accurately, even more on edge. "Alex Paige, I know your feelings for Mr. Kaine. Oh, yes, I remember you quite well, even if you didn't remember me."

"You have to admit, you do look a bit different."

Deborah straightened her spine and ran her hands down her hips, a distinctly un-William-like attempt at preening. "No matter what you think of Mr. Kaine, and what you've accused him of doing in the past - "

"For which a court of law convicted him."

"-he did not kill Nick," Deborah continued, as if Alex hadn't said a word. "It would be entirely illogical for him to do so, considering the board's approval apparently hinged on Nick's presence."

"Or on Nick not being murdered," Evelyn said.

"You said yourself you're here to find out everything you can about Nick's interaction with the board," Alex said. "What if Kaine got rid of his partner in this debacle, not realizing he was killing his golden goose?"

"That's ridiculous," Deborah scoffed.

"Is it?" Evelyn asked.

Alex decided it was time to steer the conversation back to Deborah's presence in the house. "Did you find what you were looking for?"

"Unfortunately, no. He locked his file cabinets and his laptop's password protected," she said, surprising Alex with her unembarrassed candor.

"Apparently that's a good thing," Evelyn said. "Look, Deborah, I don't know you, but Nick was my fiancé,"

"Until last night."

"That's right. You were there, weren't you? Regardless. This is Nick's home and you need to leave."

Deborah's eyes flashed pure malice, then returned to their customary cool gaze. She stood up and strode to the door, turning before exiting. "Mr. Kaine will get his golf course and his resort. He always gets what he wants."

"Not always. Not this time," Alex muttered to her back. "Wait," she said, louder. Deborah paused and turned. "You said we need you to find out who killed Nick. Why? What do you know?"

"I know that you two can't see what's right in front of you," Deborah scoffed, then sneered at Evelyn. "You don't think your boat captain is capable of murder? I saw him last night; I saw the way he protected you. He threatened Nick. And Juke wasn't the only one who had issues with him. As you said, I've worked with him for years, and I know that there are many people who would want him dead. Including, possibly, you."

Alex rolled her eyes. "On that note, isn't it time for you to leave?"

"The thing is, I also know Evelyn didn't kill him," Deborah continued, ignoring Alex. "And I have a pretty good idea who did. So don't dismiss me. Who knows, I might even be able to save your precious Mast." The door closed behind her.

"I'll give her one thing," Alex said. "She knows how to make an exit."

Evelyn crossed the room and sank into a white leather couch that matched the chaise lounge. "That woman is exhausting. How can one person be so exhausting?"

Alex started to answer when the door opened. Detective Pierce walked in, followed by William. She looked from one to the other, raising her eyebrow at her friend. He stood slightly behind the cop and eyed him up and down, then winked at her. Alex stifled a laugh by covering her mouth with her hand and looking down at the plush white carpet. Divots marked where Deborah's stilettos had been.

Billy pointed to the driveway. "Was that Ms. Minnow in the Lexus? Why was she here?"

"Yes, it was her," Evelyn answered. "She said Kaine sent her to find out about Nick's interactions with the county board."

"You let her in?"

"No," Alex responded. "She was inside when we got here."

The officer stared outside, then turned around, shut the door behind him, and checked his watch. "Those two think they can do whatever they want, don't they? I'll deal with her later. I have a feeling she's never far from Kaine."

"Billy," Evelyn said, "why are you here?"

"Looking for you. I called and it went straight to voicemail."

Evelyn pulled her phone out and checked the screen. "Oh. My battery died. I didn't realize it was so low when I called Phil," she said to Alex.

"I can't imagine why you didn't notice," Alex said wryly.

Billy walked to the white leather loveseat that was oriented perpendicular to Evelyn and sat down, resting his elbows on his knees. William followed and sat next to him, leaving a small gap between their legs. Alex raised her eyebrows slightly and William grinned, shrugged, and gave the detective a little more space. Incorrigible.

"You talked to Phil?" Billy asked. "So you know they rescheduled the vote?" Evelyn nodded. "I'm assuming you plan on being there?"

"Of course I do. Why were you looking for me? You're not going to take me in again? You know I didn't kill Nick. Wait—how'd you know I'd be here and why are you with William?"

Billy put up his right hand and began counting down his responses. "Whoa. Okay—in reverse. One: I checked to see if you were at the Mast after going to your home and I ran into this one in the lobby." He pointed his thumb at William. "He told me you two were together. Last he heard, you were heading here, and he insisted on accompanying me.

"Two: No, I am not taking you in. And three: because I need to find out anything you know about Nick's dealings with Kaine, and anyone else you think might have had it out for him."

"You didn't say you know I didn't kill him."

The detective stared at her. "Evelyn."

"Yes, yes, I know. You're just doing your job. But why is it so urgent that you drove around looking for me?"

"Because that damn fool Georgia Brannigan keeps insisting she killed Nick when we all know she didn't. I've got to find out who did, and quickly, if nothing else, so she doesn't get charged by our oh-so-eager DA. I'm holding her at bay for now, but I don't know how long she'll wait. Kaine's giving her an earful. His attorney arrived and apparently they're all golfing buddies. They're on the course right now." Billy stood up and walked toward the fireplace before turning around to lean against the wall. His shoes left imprints in the carpet, like a man walking on sand. "Georgia's lucky I'm not charging her with obstruction," Billy complained, "and for wasting my time."

"She meant well," Evelyn defended.

"Yeah, well, meaning well is the root of countless problems, if you ask me."

"What about Juke?"

"I released him before I started looking for you. He sent you a text, and when you didn't reply, he asked me to let you know he was heading to the marina." Billy addressed William and Alex. "Would you two please excuse us?"

Alex hesitated. "Go ahead," Evelyn said. They didn't move. "Really, it's fine. I've known Billy my whole life. I trust him, despite this morning," she said poignantly, then motioned down the hall. "The kitchen's at the end on the right if you want something to drink, and if you go out on the deck I'll come get you when we're done."

They reluctantly left Evelyn with the detective, William turning for one last glance before Alex pulled him down the corridor. She peered into an open door on the left, from where Deborah had emerged. Nick's office. His laptop sat open on a giant desk. Was everything he owned super-sized? The kitchen answered that question. With walls of custom cabinets, acres of granite, and a refrigerator big enough to park cars, it was exactly what she'd expect to see in a McMansion. A row of glasses sparkled above a water cooler and Alex filled two. They opened the French doors and walked outside.

"Wow," Alex gasped. "Forget the house. Give me this." The deck sat high on a bluff that rose above Lake Michigan. A steep staircase led down the side of the bluff to a dock. Even from their lofty perch, Alex and William could see through the clear water to rocks polished smooth by years of the lake's ebb, dropped in piles of muted tones. They were like precious stones in a display case.

Alex moved towards a wrought-iron table ringed with rocking chairs made of the same material. They looked distinctly uncomfortable. She noticed a deck box next to the French doors. Inside the container, she found blue and white striped cushions and arranged two on chairs facing the lake. They sat down and she eyed her friend.

"So you just happened to be in the lobby when Detective Pierce was already looking for Evelyn?"

William grinned, not looking even remotely sheepish. "Can't very well investigate much if I'm in my room, now can I?"

"Uh, huh. And just what were you investigating?"

"Well, I was hoping to investigate his fine—"

Alex raised her hands to stop him. "No, no. I do not want to know." She rocked her chair gently. "Well?" she prompted.

William began rocking as well. "I got my pitch done lickety-split, so I headed to the lobby. Someone else was waiting with me, by the way. Pecking away on his laptop. Clickity-clack. Even his typing is annoying."

Alex grunted as she stood up and walked over to the railing, leaning her elbows on the composite lumber. "Ben can wait all day, as far as I'm concerned."

"And guess who sat next to him, clickity-clacking right along with him. When she wasn't batting her eyelashes, that is."

Alex's eyes darted to William. "Harriet? With Ben? And he tolerated her?"

William nodded. "Yep. Even made him laugh a couple times. It was quite distracting. You know he laughs like a donkey?"

"Will wonders never cease," Alex said, ignoring his last comment and thinking that maybe Harriet was the answer to her Ben problem after all. "So tell me, did Detective Pierce say anything on the way over?"

"It's a short drive," William responded with a slight pout. "He didn't say a word about the case. He did, however, make small talk. Like asking me how I liked the nomadic life. He seemed rather wistful about it."

Alex turned to face him. "William Meriwether Blake, is that a crush I hear?"

"I always did like a man in uniform."

"He doesn't wear a uniform."

"But he did. Billy said he worked patrol for years before becoming a detective."

"I do declare," Alex grinned. "I thought you hated the name Billy."

"For me," William admitted. "On him? It's divine."

Chapter 13

Alex filled William in on the text messages she and Evelyn had found between Nick and Kaine, and between Nick and Phil. The door opened and Evelyn stuck her head out, letting them know Billy was leaving and he insisted they leave as well.

They followed her inside, putting their water glasses in the kitchen. As they walked out of the kitchen, Alex glanced across the hall into Nick's office, then slowed so she was trailing Evelyn and William. They walked through the front door, and before it closed behind her, Alex grabbed it. "Hey, I forgot to put the cushions away. I'll be right back." She went back into the house before Billy or Evelyn could protest, letting the door shut behind her. She raced down the hall, grabbed Nick's laptop and charging cord, exited through the French doors, and put the laptop in the deck box before covering it with the seat cushions. Her heart racing, she checked to make sure the computer and cord weren't visible. The lid dropped with a thunk.

I'm committed now, she thought ruefully. She slowed her breathing, brushed her hair back, and walked purposefully to the front door. Once Alex was back on the front steps, Evelyn entered a code on a keypad next to the frame, locking the door behind her.

Billy leaned against his Dodge Charger with his thumbs in his belt loops, waiting while the three of them climbed into Evelyn's car before getting into his own. Evelyn watched in the rearview mirror as he followed them down the long, winding driveway. "Billy warned me not to come back here until they've made an arrest."

"We need to get back in there," William said. "We need to find out what kind of deal he had with Kaine. You know the code. Think we can sneak in later?"

Evelyn shook her head. "It'll be logged, so Billy will know."

"You said you've known each other all your lives. Wouldn't he look the other way?"

Evelyn laughed. "You do remember he brought me in for questioning this morning, and I was there for hours, right? No, Nick's house is off limits."

"Alex told me you could access his text messages. Did he also back his computer up to the cloud?" he asked.

"No. He had an external drive connected to his router for backups, but that's inside his house, too. I'm afraid we're not going to get to his computer."

Alex shifted in the front seat. "Well... I might have forgotten to replace the cushions on purpose."

William reached from behind and squeezed her shoulder. "That's my girl. What'd you do?" He noticed her purse at her feet. "Your bag's not big enough and you weren't carrying it, anyway."

They turned into Evelyn's driveway, where a white Jeep with the top open waited behind Alex's car. "That's Sue's. She's probably out back," Evelyn said, then turned off the ignition and turned to Alex. "Well?"

"I might have put something in the deck box," she hedged. "Under the cushions."

Evelyn shook her head and her fingers tightened on the steering wheel. "It's a good thing Nick never hooked up the cameras that came with his alarm system, or it might be you riding in the back of Billy's car."

"You can say I did it," William said. "I'll ride in the back of his car any day."

Alex ignored him and directed a piercing look at Evelyn. "Look, I know you don't like it, but Nick had something on Phil, and I'm betting he had something on Kaine. It would explain a lot and would also explain Deborah's interest. That laptop is the only way we can find out what it is."

"You're right," Evelyn sighed. "I don't like it, but we need to find out what happened." They got out of the car and Evelyn looked across the roof at Alex. "How are you going to get it? Billy said they're going to be patrolling to make sure Deborah, or I, or you, for that matter, don't go back."

"I have some ideas. You go see Sue. I'm sure she's worried sick." Alex and William moved to her car, and she called to Evelyn before getting in. "And charge your phone."

Evelyn pulled her phone out of her back pocket and waved it before walking around the garden towards the back of the house. They settled into Alex's car and William turned to her. "Well?"

"Let's go see a man about a boat."

"Am I thinking what you're thinking?" he asked. "Please tell me we're going to see that gorgeous captain."

Alex shook her head, exasperated. "I think you've been in the wilderness too long, my friend. Weren't you just going on about Detective Pierce?"

"You've met me, right? I appreciate beauty." He rolled down his window and inhaled. "God, I love the smell of pine. Anyway, Mr. Sailor Man only has eyes for Ms. Mast."

"True. Seems they were quite the item back in the day." Alex slid her eyes towards her friend. "And Billy?"

"I'm getting a distinct vibe from him, but I won't get my hopes up. This is basically rural America, you know."

"True, but they seem pretty open here," she said, as she pulled in front of the lodge.

"Of course they do - they're wooing us so we write pretty things. You know that's how it works. But a - gasp - homosexual police officer? That's a whole different world. Even if he is, and is interested in me, which of course why wouldn't he be, I'm thinking there's little to no chance anything will come of it. And that's okay. I am happy to look and not touch." He got out of the car and walked around to the driver's side as Alex opened her door. "Speaking of looking, let's go take a gander at that other heaping spoonful of eye candy, shall we?"

Alex parked in front of the inn and they walked around the marina to Brannigan's Charters. Behind the counter, Juke leafed through a sheaf of papers. He stopped and looked up as the bells announced them. "How's Evie? Is she okay? She didn't answer her phone."

"She's fine. Her battery died. We dropped her off at home and Sue was there."

"Good. Sue's good people." He put the papers aside. "What's up?"

"Well," Alex started, "we know Evelyn's innocent - "

"Obviously."

"- and we also know time is of the essence. And, it goes without saying, but I'm going to say it anyway, that Kaine is involved. In fact, I'm pretty sure he killed Nick."

"What makes you think that?"

William took over. "Our intrepid former investigative journalist discovered that Rat Man texted Nick last night demanding he join him on the overlook at the buttcrack of dawn, and Alex here just happened to see Evelyn at the same time they were supposed to meet." He shuddered. "What is with you people and your ungodly waking habits?"

Alex ignored him, instead telling Juke about finding Nick's text messages. "How well do you know Phil?"

"Pretty well. We go fishing together quite a bit. Why?"

"Nick threatened Lindsay."

"He what?" Juke erupted. "Threatened her how?"

Alex showed him the screenshots of the exchange between Nick and Phil. Juke slumped against the wall. "So now we've got Kaine meeting with Nick, and Nick threatening Phil's daughter. Why? What did he have on him?"

"So you agree he must have been blackmailing him, then?"

"It's the only logical explanation for," Juke waved his hand with disgust at Alex's phone, "for this." He squinted at the two of them. "What's your plan?"

"Ooh, he's pretty and smart. Already knows we've got a plan," William said.

"Pretty much a no-brainer, especially since everyone else except that Harriet person has left and you two are still here. Grandma told me who you were and what you did in Chicago," he said. "Good job."

"Yes, well, not good enough." Alex looked out at the marina. "We were hoping we could rent a kayak."

Juke narrowed his eyes. "Why?"

Alex explained what she'd done with the laptop and he nodded with approval. "I'll take you there."

"No, you don't need to do that," William protested, rather weakly, Alex thought. "We don't want you to get in trouble."

"Does Evie know?"

"Yes. She knows Nick's password, so we're going to bring the laptop back to her to see if we can find out what he had on Phil, and what Deborah was so keen to find," Alex explained.

"Then I'm taking you. No argument." He looked them over. "You both look pretty fit, but the waters between here and there can get rough. Besides, kayaking'll take you a couple hours and we don't have time for that."

Juke grabbed a set of keys from the pegboard behind him under a handwritten label. They'd be taking Amelia, the same boat they'd seen him cleaning the day before, and Alex thought it must be his favorite. *Do captains have favorite boats*, she wondered. *Of course they do.* Juke began walking to the door and she put her hand up. "Look, before we go. This is awkward, but I have to ask..."

"Did I kill Nick?" Juke filled in.

Alex grimaced, looking embarrassed. "You threatened him, after all, and Evelyn told me about what happened in college."

He couldn't have rolled his eyes any harder if he'd been William. "That?" he laughed. "That was twenty years ago. Besides, I had a charter this morning."

She exhaled and relaxed her shoulders, releasing the tension she didn't realize she'd been holding. "You did?"

"Yes. Here," Juke said, and grabbed a receipt from the counter. A group of six had booked a fishing charter for six that morning. He put the white rectangle down and spread his arms wide. "Why do you think I'm here instead of at the police station? Billy confirmed the charter, and I was out." Juke put the receipt back. "You know, we do have a police department for this."

William chuckled. "That's right. You don't know Alex yet. When she gets an idea in her head, that's all she wrote. Until she writes about it." William slapped his knee, proud of his own joke.

"Well, obviously I didn't think you did it, since I told you about Phil, but I had to make sure," Alex explained.

"Especially before I take you out on the lake, right? Are you satisfied?" When she nodded, Juke turned towards the door. "I've half a mind to call Billy and tell him where the laptop is, so we better get this over with."

They followed him out to the docks. Alex's phone buzzed. *Check your email.* She put her phone in her back pocket and stepped through the open gate from the dock to the boat. "Ben," she answered William's curious glance. "He can wait."

As soon as Juke was in open water, he opened up the throttle. The hull slammed on the waves, and Alex understood why he'd thought kayaking would be a bad idea. They headed north around a small peninsula. She looked up and recognized the overlook. Was that only this morning? Within a couple of minutes, Juke slowed the boat and eased quietly into a cove. They could see the back of Nick's mansion, shaded as the sun lowered. Trees crowded the sides of the house, and Alex realized that the property was adjacent to the Nature Reserve.

"I can see why Nick would want that golf course so badly. His property values would skyrocket."

Juke agreed grimly as he deftly maneuvered the boat alongside the dock. "It wouldn't surprise me if he bought this lot with that sole intention. All he ever cared about was money. And Evie."

It was obvious to Alex that the same could be said of Juke. About Evelyn, anyway. It was equally obvious money wasn't his priority. No matter what Evelyn had said about chemistry not making a relationship, those two definitely had it.

Alex stood up. When William prepared to join her, she stopped him. "You stay here. I'll run up and grab the laptop and run right back down." She jumped onto the dock and started climbing the steep stairs. As she neared the top of the bluff, she stopped when she heard an intermittent beeping. The forest, the bluff, and the lake distorted the sound and she couldn't tell where it was coming from. Alex slowed, creeping the last few steps and peering over the edge. The French doors leading out to the deck were open. The sound was louder, and she recognized the beeps as the warning for an alarm. Whoever was inside hadn't been there long.

Now what? Alex briefly hesitated, then crouched and scrambled to the stairs leading up to the deck. She moved slowly, ever so slowly, grateful for the silent soles of her canvas tennies. The deck box was on the other side of Nick's office window. She peered inside and immediately pulled her head back. Someone was in there. She carefully glanced again and recognized Lars. He'd moved to the desk, pulling open drawers and dumping them on the floor. "No no no!" he yelled. The alarm interval shortened. It would screech any minute. Alex didn't have a choice; she ran past the window, hoping that Lars would be so distracted he wouldn't see her. She flipped open the box, extracted the laptop and power cord, and then peered quickly inside the office. Lars had his back to her, desperately moving down the row of filing cabinets, pulling on the handles as he went. None budged. Alex took a deep breath and raced to the end of the deck, scrambled down the stairs as fast as she could, hampered by the steep descent, grateful for the handrails that kept her from tumbling down. The alarm screamed across the small bay. She jumped off the last few steps, raced down the dock, and leapt into the boat. "Go go go! We have to go!" she shouted to Juke. He pulled out so quickly the propeller kicked up rocks before gaining purchase and shooting out into the bay.

Alex gulped air, collapsed into a swiveling chair, and looked back. Lars stood on the deck and watched as they pulled away, their wake slapping against the semi-circular shore. He glanced back at the house, then ran into the woods, into the Reserve, and he was gone.

"What happened? Who was that?" William asked. Juke focused on piloting.

Alex held her finger up as she caught her breath for a moment. "Lars. Lars was in Nick's office. He was looking for something, probably this," she said, and held up the computer.

"Did he see you?"

"Not up there. He was too busy ransacking the place. But he saw me down here."

"Think he recognized you? It's quite a distance from that deck down to the bay."

"Tell me about it," she wheezed. "Wow, those were a lot of stairs. I don't know, but I'd be surprised if he didn't."

"Doesn't matter. He'll know this boat, and he'll know me," Juke said, his back still turned to them.

"What do you think he'll do now?" Alex asked him.

"I have no idea."

Chapter 14

Evelyn opened the door and gestured the three of them in with a grim expression on her face. "I don't like this."

"None of us do," Alex said, "but I don't see that we had any choice."

"Sure we did. We could let Billy handle it. That's his job, after all."

"I know you trust him, but his focus is going to be on finding out who killed Nick."

"As it should be," Evelyn interrupted.

Alex put the laptop on the kitchen island, opened it, and pressed the power button. "Absolutely. But we both - all four of us - know there was something going on between Nick and Phil, and from what you said earlier, Evelyn, it sounds like Phil's vote on the Reserve was against character." She pointed at the computer. "We need to know what he had on him before the vote tomorrow and then maybe, maybe we can save The Mast."

"We could just wait for Billy to arrest Kaine. We all know he did it," William said. He grabbed an apple and took a bite. "That'll put the kibosh on the sale," he said around bites of honeycrisp.

Alex shook her head. "We can't take that chance. These things can crawl. Believe me, I know."

Juke sat down. "She's right. We've got the computer, and Alex almost got caught grabbing it, so let's see what's in it."

"What do you mean she almost got caught?" Evelyn asked.

Alex cleared her throat. "Someone was searching Nick's office when I got there."

"Who? It was Deborah, wasn't it? That conniving—"

"Lars," William blurted out. "It was Lars."

Confusion, then sorrow, flitted across Evelyn's features. "Fine," she surrendered, "Let's see what he, and Deborah, were after." She perched on the end of the chair in front of Nick's computer. Alex and William stood behind her, peering over her shoulder. She entered the password and a photo of Nick and Evelyn smiling with the lake in the background appeared.

"That's sweet," William said.

"It's when he proposed. I didn't know he'd made that his background." She shrugged it off and opened the file directory. "What am I looking for?"

"How about Nick's Blackmail Files of Doom?"

Alex lightly punched William in the shoulder. "Be serious."

Evelyn opened a folder labeled Mast. "Could it be that simple?" she wondered out loud. Several file folders appeared. "Here's one for Eliot - that's Phil. Kaine. And Dahl? What's this one?"

She opened the folder. It contained a spreadsheet and a Word document titled Emails. She opened it and the color drained from her face. "This can't be. No. I don't believe it. What was he doing?"

"What?" Alex asked.

Evelyn stared at the screen with a horrified look on her face. "It can't be," she repeated, and then sat back. "This explains so much. Oh, Lars."

"What is it?" Juke asked softly.

She held her finger up as she scrolled through the document, and then opened Nick's email program and searched for her brother's name. "I now know why we have no money," she said in shock. "Lars used our capital to cover gambling debts. Nick found out."

"How?" Alex asked.

Evelyn continued to scroll and stop, repeating the process several times. "Lars asked him for a loan. Looks like Nick said he didn't have that kind of money, but knew someone who did." She looked up at them, her eyes filled with betrayal. "Kaine."

Juke stood up and walked a few feet away, anger flowing in waves from every movement.

"Let me guess," Alex said. "Kaine learned Lars handled The Mast's finances and convinced him to use money from your accounts to pay him back. Then, when the tax bill came due, he offered a solution."

"Nefarious," William said.

"I had no choice." Lars emerged from the shadows of the hallway. He pointed a gun at them, his hand shaking violently.

"Where'd you come from?" William cried, dropping his apple and raising his hands.

Lars tipped his head to the back of the house, his eyes flitting from one of them to the other. "Door to the deck was open. I didn't want to, Evie, but I had no choice. Now give me the laptop. Please. I don't want to hurt anyone." He stretched his left hand out. The shaking of his gun hand increased until the weapon was a blur. He pulled his arm back and gripped the pistol with both hands to try to steady it. "Push it to the end of the island and step back."

Evelyn stared at her brother. "Lars, what are you doing? Why do you have grandfather's pistol? And are you seriously pointing it at me?" Her brother's head whipped to her, and he finally focused. She gestured to the laptop. "I know about the debts, about the loan. Why didn't you come to me?"

He scoffed. "And you'd do what? You'd tell me to figure it out on my own. Or tell me I never should have been gambling. That I needed help. Always little Miss Goody Two Shoes. Never does anything wrong. You'd certainly never dream of taking a risk." His voice strengthened and his hand steadied. "You'd definitely never dream of trying to improve anything. It's all the same as it was when grandfather was alive," he yelled, waving the pistol. "I did us a favor! Now The Mast will actually be something, something worth something." He foundered and stared at the gun.

"Oh, Lars," Evelyn said, her voice coated in sorrow. "So, are you going to shoot us? Are you going to shoot me?"

He looked up as if he hadn't thought of that. "What? Of course not. I just want the computer. Give me the computer and I'll go."

"Lars, please. Let's talk about this. You haven't done anything that can't be fixed."

"It doesn't need to be fixed," he protested.

"How can you say that? The Mast is gone, gone because, because... I can't believe you'd do this." Evelyn covered her face with her hands and broke down.

Pain and remorse flashed across Lars' features as he watched his sister cry. His focus entirely on her, he didn't notice as Juke sidled closer. "It'll be fine, Evie. It'll all be fine, I promise. Once we get that money, we can do whatever we want. We can go wherever we want."

Evelyn's head popped up and she aggressively wiped the tears from her face. "I *have* what I want. I don't *want* to go anywhere else."

Lars straightened, steadied his hands. "And what about me? What about what I want?" He pointed the gun at his sister. "Give me the computer, Evie."

Juke lashed out, shoving Lars' arms skyward. The gun exploded in Lars' hand and he screamed, dropping the weapon. He crumpled, writhing, gripping his hand and howling. Evelyn ran around the island, accidentally kicking the gun. It skidded towards Juke. He left it on the floor. Alex dumped the apples into the sink and filled the empty bowl with warm water. William ran to the oven and grabbed towels off the handle, throwing them at Alex. She pushed the towels into the water.

"Lars. Lars! Are you okay? Speak to me!" Evelyn cried.

Lars moaned. "My hand. My hand."

Evelyn took the wet towels from Alex and gently cleaned her brother's hand where the gun had exploded, tears pouring down her cheeks and splashing on his shirt. "This gun hasn't been touched in years. What were you thinking?" She turned to Juke. "Call an ambulance. Why haven't you called an ambulance?"

"It'll take too long. I'll drive him."

"Lars, can you get up? We're going to take you to the hospital, okay?"

"Evie. I'm sorry," Lars gasped. He moaned. "It just went off. I never would have shot you." His voice weakened.

"Sshhh. We'll take care of you," she comforted. Juke came over and the two helped him up. He screamed in pain and collapsed, but Juke caught him and carried him towards the front door, Evelyn close behind.

Alex and William watched them, knowing they'd been forgotten. Alex hated to say something, but they didn't have a car since Juke had driven them from the marina. As Evelyn reached the door, she turned and noticed them. She grabbed the keys from the basket and threw them to William. "Here. Take my car. And take the computer with you. We need to keep it safe." She ran after Juke and Lars, leaving the door wide open.

Alex stared after them, then turned to William. "I'm going to clean this up," she said morosely, motioning to the pool of blood on the floor. "I don't want Evelyn to come back to this."

William stared at the front door. "Don't you think we should call the police?" and shifted his gaze to look pointedly at the gun.

"I don't know," she said, sounding lost. "I don't know what to do."

William hugged her, holding her close. "This is definitely not what we signed up for, is it?"

Alex grunted. "Not even close." She pulled a towel from the bowl and squeezed out the excess water. "I'll start on this. Will you lock the back door?"

"On it." William pivoted and walked away. "And then I need a drink. Or twelve!" he shouted from down the hall.

Alex put the laptop in a canvas bag she'd found in a kitchen drawer and they drove Evelyn's forest green Outback to The Mast. They ran the computer up to Alex's room and she double-checked that she'd locked the balcony door. She really would have preferred staying in her room and digging into those files, but

William was so upset he didn't say a word on the way over. He wouldn't leave her side, and when she held his hand to comfort him, she felt it shaking. She wasn't immune to the stress they'd just endured, either. Alex might have covered murder scenes and criminals in the past, but she'd never had someone point a gun at her. *He didn't point it at you*, Alex admonished herself. *But he pointed it in my general direction. Oh great. Now I'm having a conversation with myself. Maybe I do need a drink.* They walked over to the Rowdy Cormorant. As they neared, they heard music coming from inside the bar.

"Sounds like Georgia's been sprung," Alex said. When they opened the door, they discovered she was correct. There Georgia was on stage, belting out a bluesy version of Johnny Cash's *In the Jailhouse*.

Alex and William found the last seats at the bar and ordered Old Fashioneds. They simultaneously took a big drink and leaned back in their chairs, and looked up at the ceiling. William exhaled and looked to the stage as the band took their set break. His eyes narrowed. "Oh crap. Not again."

"What?" Alex turned to follow William's gaze and saw Ben approaching. "Crap is right." He walked right up to her, stopping six inches from her barstool.

"Did you check your email?" Ben asked.

"What? Oh, that. I completely forgot about your text."

"Check it."

"Ben, I am not in the mood for any of your games. Since you're standing right here, why don't you tell me instead?"

"Because it requires discretion." He eyed the man sitting next to Alex and then laughed at the expression of disbelief on her face. "No, not that. This is about what's happening here," he pointed to the ground, "in Alvin's Landing. I found something."

"Is this man bothering you?" Georgia had made her way to the bar, the bass player close behind her, and was looking over Ben's shoulder at Alex.

Alex gave a small smile. "Thanks, Georgia. Ben, I'll look at it later, okay? Now I've had a very, very long day. I know how to get in touch with you if I have any questions."

"Yes, you do. Don't worry about the time. I'm always up for middle-of-the-night texts from you." She watched Ben walk back to the end of the bar and tap a man on his shoulder, pointing to the drink covered with a napkin. The man glared at Ben, but he got up. Ben sat down and lifted his drink, giving Alex a long-distance cheers.

"He sure is full of himself, isn't he?" Georgia said, her distaste obvious.

"You have no idea," William answered. "Did you make a break for it? How'd you get out?"

The bass player, a clean cut slim man of indeterminate age with a pompadour and black-rimmed glasses, put a possessive arm around her. "Because she was with me this morning."

"Gabe here found out I'd turned myself in and made a beeline for the station." Georgia leaned into him. "I'd been trying to keep our little fling secret since there's somewhat of an age difference, but he had other ideas."

"There's no 'little fling' about it, Ms. Brannigan," the bassist said.

"If anybody's going to be a cougar, it should be you," William said, "and I mean that in the nicest way."

Georgia acknowledged him with a tip of her head. "Evelyn's out, so I got what I wanted. Now we just have to nail that Kaine. I may not have been Nick's biggest fan, but he didn't deserve to be killed. You'll get him," she said to Alex and turned without a word. Gabe grinned and turned to follow.

"Good for them," William said, then tapped Alex's phone. "Think you should check your email?"

Alex sighed, but she opened her email program and scrolled until she found Ben's message. She read it, then looked up at the rows of liquor on the back bar without really seeing them. She absentmindedly handed the phone to William.

He quickly skimmed the email and whistled softly. "Think this is it? What Nick had on Phil?"

"Possibly. Makes sense." She got up and walked over to Ben, then motioned William to join them at an empty table in the very front of the lounge near the door.

Chapter 15

Alex sat in a chair facing the room and scooted away when Ben moved a little too close. She read the email again. He'd sent her several newspaper clippings, the first from twenty-two years ago. A young woman named Olivia Prescott, home from college during summer break, had been found dead on a rocky beach on the Green Bay side of the peninsula. Phillip Eliot, her boyfriend, was the primary suspect, or at least he was until Nicholas Langley provided an alibi.

Future clippings followed Phil. When he returned to school, he began volunteering at the conservation areas local to his college. In an interview highlighting his service upon his graduation, he said he did it for Olivia. "Listen to this," Alex said. "'Her one passion was the environment,' according to Phil." She scrolled. "Seems like he followed her path. Interning with the DNR, serving on countless environmental boards. He even co-authored legislation that created four more county parks.

"And get this: last summer he talked about folding the Alvin's Landing Nature Reserve into Green Bay National Wildlife Refuge."

She put her phone down. "It makes no sense that he'd spend two decades championing Mother Nature and then vote to give away the Reserve. Did you know there are three unique ecosystems contained within its borders?"

William nodded. "My editor and I discussed that this afternoon. That's the angle he wants me to work on."

"It makes no sense," Ben echoed, "until you get to that last article." Say what she wanted about him; he knew how to dig up stories.

Alex read the headline aloud: "County Board Chairman Phillip Eliot Endorses Nicholas Langley for Village President."

"And where Phil goes, the county follows," Sue interjected from the table next to theirs. She got up and sat in the empty chair at their table.

"Oh, hello Sue. I didn't see you," Alex said.

"I could tell." She leaned forward and spoke quietly. The three of them imitated her movement so they could hear her. "The whole situation was awful. Olivia was simply lovely. A joy to be around. Phil was head over heels, and anyone who knew them knew that he'd never hurt her. They finally ruled it an accident after Nick gave Phil an alibi. Still, rumors circulated for years."

"Looks like he got past those rumors, considering he's now the County Board Chairman," Ben pointed out.

"It was twenty years ago," Sue reminded him. "Sounds like you've done your research, so you can see he's done a lot of good for this county. For the state. Besides, people have short memories and Phil inspires loyalty." She stopped at Ben's sneer. "Not like that. He's one of the good ones. He's like that favorite professor, you know? Everybody wants to sit in the front of the class. Almost everybody."

Sue pointed to Alex's phone. "What those articles won't tell you is that up until Olivia died, Phil and Nick were thick as thieves. Then Phil went back to school in Madison, Nick followed Evelyn to Chicago, and as far as I could tell, they didn't talk to each other again until Nick showed up a few years ago."

"How would you know whether or not they talked?" Ben asked incredulously.

Sue gave him a scathing frown. "You're not from a small town, are you? They'd both come back every Christmas. I noticed that first year that Phil was never at a party if Nick was there, and I didn't see them together until Nick moved back a few years ago. It was quite unexpected when Phil endorsed him for Village President."

Ben kicked back in his chair, rocking on two legs. "Seems pretty obvious to me what happened."

Alex filled in the blanks. "Phil either killed Olivia, or knew what happened, and Nick lied for him," she said. "That would certainly give him some leverage."

"Bingo," Ben agreed, pointing his finger at Alex like a gun. After what had happened earlier, she shivered.

"It certainly provides a motive, too," William said.

Sue vigorously shook her head. "Not Phil," she objected. "I don't know exactly what happened to Olivia, but I know Phil wouldn't have hurt her. Her death devastated him."

"And Nick? Would he hurt him?" Ben asked.

"I don't believe it. Phil's simply not capable of murder."

"You'd be surprised what people will do," Alex said. "Especially when they're threatened, and Nick threatened Lindsay."

Ben raised his eyebrows. Sue started. "He did? That rotten..." She stopped herself. "Who told you that?"

"My question exactly," Ben said.

Alex brushed them off. While some people might forget that she was a writer, she would never forget that Ben was a reporter, although she'd already said too much. She didn't want any of this getting out and she knew he'd use whatever information he could to write attention-grabbing headlines. At this point, it was all supposition and rumor, but she at least knew Ben had enough ethics to hold off until he could verify his suspicions.

Ben drummed his fingers on the table. "It doesn't fit. Sue, you seem to know Phil pretty well. Would he have tried to set Evelyn up for Nick's murder?"

"What?" Sue reacted like she'd been slapped. "No. Never. Why would you even think that?"

Before Alex could stop him, Ben answered. "Because someone sent her a text message from Nick's phone more than an hour after he was dead asking her to meet him at the overlook at nine, which is exactly when this group," he waved his fingers at Alex and William, "were supposed to arrive during Kaine's tour."

"So they confirmed the time of death?" Alex asked.

"Yes," Ben replied. "Between 6:10 and 6:30 this morning."

"Was that only this morning?" William groaned. "Gawd, this has been a long day."

Sue was shaking her head. "Phil couldn't have known what time we'd be at the overlook. Kaine sprung his change of plans on me last night. Only he, Deborah, Lars, and I knew this morning's full schedule."

William inhaled as if to speak, but Alex gave him a quelling look and he closed his mouth. She knew he was about to tell them how Nick was blackmailing Evelyn's brother, and that Lars was now in the hospital because he'd tried to shoot them. News of that escapade would make Ben positively gleeful.

"It's Kaine then. It must be Kaine," she said.

"Alex, I know you really, really want it to be Kaine, but the first rule of investigative reporting is to investigate,"

Ben scoffed. "Or have you already forgotten the basic tenets while you traipse around the country for your little blog?"

She simmered, but she knew better than to engage him. "Sue, thank you. It's good to know that Phil most likely—"

"Didn't," Sue interjected.

"—had nothing to do with killing Nick." She pushed her chair back and stood up. "You'll be at the board meeting tomorrow?"

"Yes," Sue replied

"I'll see you then." Alex walked out and heard William thank Sue before scrambling after her. He, too, ignored Ben.

"You're welcome!" her ex shouted.

Early the next morning, Alex opened her eyes and fumbled for her phone. She used the light from the screen to find the clothes she'd set out before she went to bed. After the previous day, she needed her early morning routine like an addict needs a fix. She needed the hit she got from feeling the grass, the sand, the rippling water, and watching a new day begin.

Yesterday had begun with a curious see-saw of determination and excitement. While she was excited to be traveling again, to be exploring a new destination, Kaine's presence and the danger he presented brought back her old commitment to right the world's wrongs. Despite chucking her reporting for a career that was more fulfilling, as she admitted to William, she did sometimes miss the thrill.

Not this kind of thrill, though. Only once before had she been intimately involved with a murder. It was her last crime beat assignment before she moved to investigative reporting. Until then, no matter how many bodies she'd seen, and over five years she'd seen more than her share, she'd remained detached. Now here she was again. Investigating a murder. And potentially, hopefully, putting a loathsome man behind bars, again, with the bonus of helping to save a place worth saving.

Alex walked down the stairs and to the beach slowly, taking her time, pulling every moment like taffy. The first hint of sun broke over the horizon, a bright yellow reminiscent of a rain slicker. She pictured the Morton salt girl, with her umbrella and her boots, even though the sky was clear. It looked to be a beautiful day, with no repeat of yesterday's gale.

A sign? This afternoon the board would vote on the Reserve's, and possibly, The Mast's, fate. At least its immediate fate, since Kaine probably wouldn't want the inn if he couldn't build his golf course. Even if Evelyn could hold on to it, the question would be for how long. The taxes would still be due, and after last night's revelation of blackmail, betrayal, and possible false alibis, she knew today would be a mixed bag.

Then there was Kaine. Why hadn't Billy arrested him yet? She smiled at the thought of William's reaction to the detective, but then directed her thoughts back to the murder. The scenario played out in her head: Kaine sent Nick a text message the night before; he lured him to the overlook, killed him, then sent a text from Nick's phone to frame Evelyn. Nefarious, as William said. They hadn't gotten to Nick's file on Kaine before Lars barged in brandishing a gun, but she had a feeling Nick was demanding a bigger piece of the pie than Kaine wanted to divvy up and he jumped the gun, so to speak, killing him too soon.

It fit. It fit with what she knew about Kaine and what she'd learned about Nick. The question was, how to prove it? The first thing she had to do was look at those files on Nick's laptop. Then she'd talk to Phil. Once she eliminated him as a suspect, that would only leave Kaine. This time, she'd make sure he paid for the lives he'd ruined.

Alex closed her eyes and counted to six as she inhaled, then again as she exhaled. A cool breeze ruffled her short hair and she wrapped her arms around her chest. When she opened her eyes, the sun had risen to a half-circle and was so bright she had to look away.

Chapter 16

"Room service."

Alex closed the laptop and answered the door. The young man she'd seen in the gazebo the day she arrived—was that only two days ago?—wheeled in a cart. He wore jeans and a polo with The Mast's logo on it. *That's one of the things Kaine will change*, she thought. *They'll all be trussed up in tuxes.* She directed him to the balcony and he placed a bowl of fruit and a plate with a bagel, cream cheese, capers, tomatoes, and a giant mound of smoked salmon on the table. Before leaving, he poured her a cup of coffee from the pitcher and she could smell the cherries. That ubiquitous quirk was definitely something she'd include in her story.

Her story. She realized it was the first time she'd thought concretely of writing, which for Alex was like forgetting to breathe. When she'd told William the day before that she had an idea of how to help Evelyn save the inn, if they could wrestle it back from Kaine in the first place, she was thinking of the story she would write, but it was a nascent idea, nothing solid. Now the words began to take shape: she would tell their history, the passion, the friendliness of everyone she'd met, with the exception of a few. She hadn't been too keen on Nick, and Lars wasn't exactly someone she'd invite to dinner, but everyone else had been wonderful.

Alex was invested. She wanted to help, and the only way she could was through words. As a reporter, she'd wielded them as weapons from her arsenal. As a travel writer, they became powerful tools of inspiration that helped her readers create memories. When this was done, when Kaine was in jail, again, and The Mast was safe, Alex would write the best article she'd ever written and her readers would flock to this special place.

She spread cream cheese on the bagel, then placed a strip of salmon on top, piled some capers and tomatoes, and cut off a bite. She chewed while opening the laptop again and found the email exchanges between Nick and Kaine. They were what she'd expected, although Kaine was much more articulate via the written word. That surprised her; the man had a third-grade vocabulary, and here he was flinging about college-level words. Reading their interplay of threats and greed put Alex's stomach off the salmon and she set it aside. Unfortunately, there was no smoking gun, no blackmail. Instead, Nick's tactic was simple coercion: he'd convince his fiancé to sell to the developer and he would ensure the County Supervisors Board voted in favor of converting the Reserve to a golf course—but only if he got a considerable piece of the puzzle.

Kaine balked, of course, but Nick had worked with him enough to know he always undercut his partners, and he was prepared. With what exactly, she didn't know. After threatening to pull his support entirely, he ended his last email with a cryptic salvo: "Remember. I know what you did. I know where the bodies are buried."

Was that metaphorical, she wondered, or had Kaine murdered others? She wouldn't put it past him. A key witness, a contractor who'd worked with him on the failed Gold Coast development, had been murdered in a botched burglary right before the trial. "Conveniently" murdered, Alex always thought. His testimony would have put Kaine away for years. Now that was someone who'd known where the bodies were buried. He'd begged for protection, but the police ignored his requests. Kaine was a heavy contributor to their fraternity.

Alex determined words would be Kaine's undoing, once again. The one person who would know everything would be Deborah. She'd have to find a way to get the woman alone, and then somehow break whatever hold her boss had on her and get her to explain what Nick meant. Ha! she laughed at herself. That woman would be more likely to wear jeans and a t-shirt than she would be to betray Kaine—and Alex doubted Deborah had a single item made of denim or cotton in her entire wardrobe.

She wanted to call William. He often saw things she didn't, but the night before he'd told her that no way, no how was he getting up before ten so she better not even think of waking him, unless, of course, they were going to go see Billy or Juke.

Alex wrapped the rest of the salmon in a napkin to take to Alvin on her way out. It was no wonder that cat was so fat. She set it aside and opened the file labeled Eliot.

Alex pulled up to a low-slung ranch with horizontal lines. It looked like one of Frank Lloyd Wright's Usonian homes, but she didn't know if the architect had designed any in this area. She admired the way it blended into the woods so skillfully that she would have driven right by if it weren't for the upright red flag on the mailbox at the end of the driveway.

She rang the doorbell and a teenage girl with braces answered the door. "Ms. Paige!" she cried. "What are you doing here?" She peered around Alex's shoulder. "Is Ms. Dahl with you? I heard what happened to Mr. Langley. Is she okay?"

"Hi, Lindsay," Alex said after a brief moment to collect herself. She hadn't expected to see her. "No, she's not with me, and she's doing as well as can be expected, I suppose. I'm actually hoping to speak to your father. Is he around?"

A man with prominent cheekbones and mahogany skin appeared behind Lindsay. He put his hand on his daughter's shoulder and she stiffened. "May I help you?"

"Mr. Eliot? I'm Alex Paige. I'm one of the writers in town for the press trip."

"I thought all of you would have left after what happened."

"Obviously not, Dad." Lindsay rolled her eyes, her tone scornful.

He glanced sadly at his daughter and opened the door wide. "Please come in," he said, gesturing Alex inside. "Hon, we're going to sit out back. Would you mind bringing us a pitcher?"

Lindsay glared at her dad. "Fine," she said.

Alex followed Phil towards the back of the house. "Out back" was essentially another room, with a massive grill as the highlight of an outdoor kitchen furnished with rattan chairs and couches with dark red cushions, and a high-top table surrounded by tall barstools. In the yard, benches circled a fire pit and butterflies swarmed a grove of milkweed. "This is incredible," she said.

"Thanks." He sat down on one of the couches. "Have a seat."

A hiss of air escaped as she sank into the thick all-weather cushion. Lindsay came out and put a tray of iced tea and a plate of chocolate chip and cherry cookies on the table between them, and her father filled Alex's glass with the red beverage. "It's the cherries," he explained.

"Evelyn filled me in on the cherry obsession. It's definitely a selling point." She watched Lindsay walk back inside. "She's a lovely young woman."

Phil smiled, his pride touched with sorrow. "Inside and out. We're very proud of her." He took a bite of cookie and pushed a bit of cherry into his mouth. "We being her mother, Rose, and I."

"I hope you don't mind my saying so, but she seems a little upset with you."

He laughed abruptly, choking a bit on his cookie. "Well, you certainly don't mess around, do you?" He smiled, taking the edge off his words.

"You'll have to forgive me. I spent many years as a reporter," she said.

"And old habits die hard?"

Alex lifted her shoulders, a slight shrug. "Honestly? I've been a lot less hard-hitting in recent years, but with what's happened here... " She trailed off.

"You're thrown back into the fray, as it were," he finished for her. He smoothed a finger over a crease in his jeans. "Let's just say Lindsay is none too pleased with Mr. Kaine's plans for the Reserve."

Alex took a cookie as well, biding her time with chocolate and cherries. She hadn't entirely thought through how she'd approach the man, but Lindsay's presence, and obvious disappointment in her father, had opened the door.

"That's actually why I'm here." When he raised an eyebrow, she continued. "No, not about Lindsay. I was curious about the Reserve. From what I've heard, it's uncharacteristic that you would vote to let it become a golf course." She said it as gently as she could because she expected him to get defensive after what she'd learned about him and his history of dedication to protecting the environment.

"Yes, I've definitely not followed my normal path," he admitted.

"It seems like you've been fighting for the environment for years. You alone created four county parks."

He chuckled. "I certainly didn't do that by myself. There was lots of support and many people were involved."

"Fair enough." Alex put the rest of her cookie down on a napkin. "But you were the driving force. And last year you proposed incorporating the Reserve into the National Wildlife Refuge."

Phil sat back and tilted his head, appraising her. "You've done your research."

"As you said..."

"Old habits die hard." He ate the last bite of his cookie and swallowed. "Why don't you ask what you came here to ask."

Alex considered the contained man across from her. He exuded strength. Yet despite his kindly demeanor, sorrow hovered as she figured out how to ask him what she wanted to know. She decided on one word.

"Olivia."

He stared at her, then collapsed inwards, curling in on himself, becoming smaller. His eyes focused on the iced tea pitcher, following a single bead of condensation as it dripped down the side of the silver ewer to the table. He raised his head and gazed over her shoulder, but Alex knew the only thing he saw was what had happened twenty-two years before.

"I wondered when," he started. "I thought, maybe, with Nick gone, but he'd saved everything, our correspondence, right?" Alex dipped her chin with the smallest of motions, afraid any drastic movement would distract him. She watched, motionless, while he took a deep breath and gathered the courage to talk about something he'd kept hidden for two decades.

"We were home from school," he started. "It was our first summer break. I hadn't seen Olivia in a couple months. I'd gone to Madison and she went to the University of Iowa. She wanted to be a writer," he explained, his voice monotone at first, but warming as he spoke. "She dreamed of being accepted to the Iowa Writers Workshop. Every time I'd visit her, she'd take me to another place where a famous author had been. Her favorite was the house where Kurt Vonnegut lived.

"Neither one of us could get away after spring break, and when we both got back home, I couldn't wait to see her, but she kept putting me off. I, God, I was so stupid." He put his head in his hands. When he looked up, he met Alex's eyes directly. "I thought she'd met someone. She finally agreed to see me, so we went to our favorite spot."

"Sunset Point."

"Yes. Have you been yet?" When Alex shook her head, he continued. "The view is mesmerizing; there's a reason for its name. That was our place. It was a lot of people's place, but we felt like it was ours. I bought flowers, planned to do anything I could to get her back."

"Had she broken up with you?" Alex asked.

"Not specifically, but she was taking longer and longer to return my calls. Same thing with my texts. She explained she was running out of data."

"Ah, pre-unlimited plans. I remember those days," Alex said.

Phil agreed. "It was all very logical. But then I saw her, and she was so sad, and so distant, I just knew she was breaking up with me."

"What did you do?"

He started. "Not that! I accused her of seeing someone else. She looked at me like I'd slapped her and ran off. I didn't chase her. I didn't follow her. If I had… "

Alex waited while he gathered himself. He lowered his eyes to the ground again and spoke softly. "Instead, I left. I drove around for hours, until I finally went to Nick's. He gave me a couple shots of Jack and opened a twelve pack and we drank every one of them. The next morning, the cops were banging on his door. They were going to arrest me, said they knew I'd been with Olivia the night before. I didn't know what happened. I asked over and over and they wouldn't tell me until finally they said that she, that she was dead.

"It was incomprehensible. My worst nightmare," he whispered. "I was going to ask her to marry me. Instead, I was a damn fool. She ran off." He looked up, his eyes haunted. "It's my fault she died."

"What happened?" Alex prompted, when he stopped, lost in his memories.

"Nick gave me an alibi. Swore up and down that he'd been with me all night. Said Olivia'd been 'blowing me off,' so I did the same to her. I wish I had. She'd probably still be alive."

"Mr. Eliot—"

"Please, I think we're beyond the formal stage,: he said sadly.

"Phil, it doesn't sound like it's your fault. Why didn't you come forward?"

He straightened and his chocolate eyes bore into hers. "Olivia was white."

Chapter 17

"Would that really have mattered?"

Phil clenched his lips. "Yes," he said simply.

Alex waited.

"Her parents didn't care. Beautiful people. Kind people. But not everyone is like them. As a teenager I'd been pulled over so many times for supposed traffic violations I considered giving up driving altogether." Phil's hands gripped each other so tightly the color disappeared from his knuckles. "We started dating our senior year in high school and she'd find nasty, cruel notes taped to her locker. I offered to break up, for her sake, and she'd laugh and tell me I was being ridiculous.

"But I wasn't. People can be cruel, especially when somebody does something that doesn't fit their worldview. So when Olivia died," his voice caught again, "and Nick said I'd be the first and only suspect, I knew he was right. Any time I thought about coming forward, he'd remind me that nobody would believe that I'd left her there. I had no alibi. Nick gave me one. He saved me, and he saved my parents and my sister from having to go through that. Because you know—" his eyes were piercing, "—

you know full well that I would have been arrested and convicted.

"This?" Phil gestured. "All of this? Would never have happened if Nick hadn't lied for me. I wouldn't have finished school. Wouldn't have met Rose. Wouldn't have Lindsay. I owe Nick everything."

Alex spoke without moving, afraid to break the spell. "When did he decide to collect?"

Phil shifted his gaze to the screened door behind Alex and started. "Lindsay—how much have you heard?"

His teenage daughter came outside. She'd changed into the jeans and polo uniform of The Mast. The cushion exhaled as she sat next to Alex. "Enough. Dad, was Mr. Langley blackmailing you?" her voice incredulous.

He chuckled nervously. "*Blackmail* is such a strong word, isn't it? It feels so… ominous. Which, I suppose it is, since I was about to betray myself, betray Olivia, and betray you," he said to Lindsay. "It didn't seem like much at first. After that summer, Nick and I went our separate ways. I could never bring Olivia back, so I did everything I could to honor her, but in the back of my mind, I always wondered. I knew my freedom, my life was based on a lie. But I didn't hear from him, and over the years that feeling dissipated, especially when I met your mom." Phil gave his daughter a small smile.

"The lie was his, though," Alex said. "Nick committed perjury, so he also had something to lose."

"Honestly? That didn't even cross my mind. Growing up, Nick was the golden boy. The quintessential cliché. Football star, prom king, valedictorian. And he chose me as his best friend, stood up for me when I was scrawny." He stopped at the shocked looks on their faces and laughed a little. "Yes, I was scrawny, as hard as that may be to believe."

He looked from one to the other. "And then he lied for me, to save me, because he knew I didn't hurt Olivia. He believed in me.

"So, yes, I felt like I owed him. When he came back after Evelyn got cancer and asked for my endorsement for Village President, I willingly gave it to him. I knew he wanted to impress her, and the one sure way to impress Evelyn Dahl is to care about her home."

"But Dad, I don't understand," Lindsay said, and stood up. "What about the Reserve? How could you destroy the Reserve for a stupid golf course? That was our place, our favorite place." She strode to the end of the deck and watched the butterflies.

Phil turned and spoke to her back. "I was scared," he admitted. "I was afraid of the same thing that scared me twenty-two years ago. What if they thought I hurt her? What if they didn't believe me? Why would they? We'd kept the lie going for over two decades. Everything I've done that's good for this county would be tainted, it would be ruined."

Lindsay whipped around. "It's ruined now! Don't you see that? If Mr. Langley hadn't been murdered, you'd just go ahead and vote for that stupid golf course and the whole place would be ruined forever." She started towards the door and her father stood in front of her, placing his hands gently on her shoulders. She buckled, crying. "Dad, how could you? How could you?" she pleaded.

Alex sat, forgotten, as Phil wrapped his arms around his daughter. "I'm sorry, my sweet girl. I am so sorry." He pulled back and tipped her chin up with his finger. "I'm going to go to the police right now and tell them what happened with Olivia, okay?"

Lindsay's head whipped up and she stepped back from him. "No! No. You're going to go to that meeting this afternoon and you are going to vote no on that golf course and you are going to save the Reserve. Then you can go to the cops."

Phil put his hands up against her passionate onslaught. "You're right. You're absolutely right."

His daughter searched his face. "You need to tell Mom first," she said.

"I will. She'll be home soon and I'll talk to her then. She's been pretty upset with me, too."

"Well, you've been an idiot."

With that statement, Lindsay walked back into the house, ignoring Alex on her way out. Phil watched the door as it closed behind his daughter, then returned to the couch.

"Looks like I've got my marching orders," he said.

"You most certainly do. That's one heck of a daughter you've got there, Mr. Eliot."

"No doubt about that." He leaned his elbows on his knees. "Did that answer your questions?"

Alex considered him. His features had relaxed. A burden had been lifted. "It's going to be okay, you know."

"No, I don't," he said sadly, "but I appreciate you saying so. Things are different now. Talking to my wife is not going to be fun," he added.

"If she's anything like your daughter, I think you'll be just fine," Alex said, then stood up. She reached her hand out and he stood up as well and shook it.

She watched the horizontal lines of the house grow distant in her rearview mirror. Phil had a powerful motive for killing Nick, especially after he'd threatened Lindsay, but she agreed with Sue: that man was not a killer. After calling Evelyn to confirm she was home, she called William and told him she was going to pick him up. She needed to tell them both what she'd learned, about Phil and about Kaine. She checked the dashboard clock. They had four hours before the meeting. Would that be enough time?

"My word. You've been up for hours, haven't you, Ms. Early Bird?" William said as he got in the front seat with a flourish. He smelled of ocean, or at least what the fragrance manufacturers considered the smell of the ocean. It was his signature and Alex loved it. She leaned over and sniffed him.

"Hmmmm. You smell nice."

"Are you seriously sniffing me?"

"You know me—I've got a 'nose' for things," she grinned, and followed the driveway out to the road and headed south towards Evelyn's cabin.

"Oh boy," William groaned. "You're in an awfully good mood."

"Yes, I am, and for good reason."

"Do tell, fair lady. To what do we owe the pleasure of your pleasure?"

She pulled to a stop, turned off the engine, and smiled sideways at her friend. "I will reveal all once we're inside, but let's just say I think someone may finally get his due."

William opened his door and jumped out. She shook her head; he even rushed gracefully. "Then stop dilly-dallying and get on with it," he said. Alex grabbed the laptop from the back seat and followed him to the door. He pushed the doorbell several times and Evelyn answered the insistent ringing.

"Yes, yes, I'm here." She looked from one to the other as they filed inside. "I take it you found something?"

"She did, but she wouldn't tell me until we were with you." William sat on a barstool at the island and grabbed a honeycrisp. Evelyn had replaced the bowl from last night with a different one. He pointed the apple at Alex. "Spill."

Alex put the laptop on the counter and gestured to it. She explained that she'd gone through Nick's files that morning and told them about Phil's confession. Evelyn's face fell and Alex dialed back her excitement.

"How could I not have seen what kind of person Nick was?" Evelyn asked. "I had no idea he was capable of any of this."

"You strike me as the kind of person who sees the best in everyone, and I'm sure Nick presented what he knew you wanted to see."

"Thanks, Alex. That's kind of you, but I still should have had some idea." Evelyn sat next to William in front of the laptop. "So, what did you find?"

Alex reached around her to open the folder labeled Kaine and gave them a summary of Nick's duplicity: he'd convince Evelyn to sell and he'd make sure the board would vote for the golf course, and in return, he wanted a significant payoff. Phil wasn't the only board member to get Nick's special brand of blackmail; it seemed two others were having an affair with each other and he threatened to tell their spouses.

William emitted a low whistle. "He was a real piece of work, wasn't he?" Alex nudged him and glanced at Evelyn, and he had the grace to look slightly abashed before continuing. "I wonder how he got the goods on so many people?"

"He was charming, when he wanted to be, and people took him into their confidence," Evelyn said, then looked at Alex. "He had a gift not dissimilar to yours.

I still can't believe how much I told you when I'd just met you."

"Yes, well, the difference is Alex would never be so slimy," William defended his friend.

"I didn't mean that. I'm afraid my words aren't going to come out the right way."

"Don't worry about it. You've been through a lot," Alex said, patting Evelyn's hand in a distinctly maternal gesture. She scrolled to the end of the emails and stopped at the phrase that had struck her that morning. "This is what I wanted to show you. I don't think Nick was being metaphorical."

William read a portion of it out loud. "Bodies are buried, eh? You think he's speaking literally?"

Alex nodded. "Yes, I do." She explained about the contractor. "He was going to be a key witness. When he was killed, somebody ransacked his office and stole the ledger and files, as well as his computer. The information he was supposed to provide would have put Kaine away for a very, very long time, not the wrist slap he ended up getting."

"And if he's killed once..." William said.

"Exactly. For all we know, he's got a whole string of bodies of people who got in his way."

"I still don't understand why he would have killed Nick before the vote."

Alex shrugged. "Kaine is impulsive. Greed consumes him."

"What about these two?" William squinted at the screen. "Doug and Trixie, the ones having an affair."

Evelyn shook her head. "No, their relationship isn't exactly secret. It's pretty common knowledge that they're each in a bad marriage, to the point they're both separated."

"I'm getting the impression this isn't Mayberry around here," William observed.

"No place is," Alex said. "Kaine wouldn't have known that, though."

"True," Evelyn said, "but he's getting their vote another way. He promised Doug the contract for the golf course landscaping and told Trixie he wouldn't charge rent her first year if she opened a second boutique location in his resort." When Alex raised an eyebrow, Evelyn continued. "Juke and Doug are fishing buddies. Have been since they were kids. He was excited about the work, said he'd need it to pay for his divorce attorney. He felt like Kaine's plans would mean he and Trixie could finally be together." She stopped. "It's amazing what people will tell each other out on the water."

Alex turned her wrist to check the time. They had a couple of hours before the meeting. "If Phil sticks to his guns, he'll be voting against the golf course today. That's going to make Kaine furious." She looked pointedly at Evelyn. "I think you need to be prepared, possibly consider staying with Sue, or Juke."

"Isn't there enough to arrest him?" William said. He started to throw out his apple core when Evelyn pointed him towards a compost bin in a cabinet along the wall.

"Who knows? You could always call Billy and ask him," Alex said, with an impish grin.

"Don't tempt me. What do you really think's going to happen today?" They both looked at Evelyn.

Chapter 18

Evelyn sat back with a pensive look on her face and considered before answering. "Honestly, I don't know, but after what you said about Phil, I think the vote will be in our favor. Kaine will erupt, but there's nothing he can do. There's no process for appeal. He might go through with the purchase, though, just to be vindictive. From what you've said about him, and the interactions I've had, I wouldn't put it past him."

Alex was nodding. "Yes, that's exactly what he'd do. He's definitely the type to think if he can't have what he wants, then no one should." She put her hands on her thighs and pushed herself up out of the barstool. "This has been a pretty intense morning and I need some time to myself to think, so I'm going to head back to The Mast for a bit." She gave Evelyn a small hug and motioned William to join her as she started towards the door. "We'll see you this afternoon, okay?"

William waited until they were in Alex's car to speak. "Do you think I should call Billy?"

"I don't think he'd tell you anything."

"You'd be surprised..."

"Ha! Not in the slightest. I do know how charming you can be."

"Can be?" he asked incredulously. "Don't you mean how charming I am?"

"Yes, yes, my mistake."

"I'll use the text messages as a pretext. See if he knows about them. I can fill him in on the blackmail attempts, too."

"No!" Alex said sharply. "Then he'll know we've had Nick's computer."

"He could just assume that Evelyn had it. They were engaged, after all."

Alex sighed. "Just be careful what you tell him, okay? I don't want anything to jeopardize making Kaine pay for this."

"Darling, I'm charming, remember? I've got this." They pulled into a parking spot at The Mast next to William's campervan.

"I'm going to take Bessie into the Reserve and work from there. She and I both need a little forest bathing. I'll be back with plenty of time before we have to leave," he said, then climbed into the driver's seat of his van.

After he pulled out, only four cars remained in the parking lot; all the guests were taking advantage of the beautiful weather. The hotel hadn't been overflowing, but there had been steady business. She'd seen a few families, a few couples, groups of fishing buddies and that morning a bachelorette party had been checking in when she left to drive to Phil's. It was a strong mix of clientele, and she knew it would be even busier over the weekend. This was a happy place, an affordable getaway.

So much was riding on the vote this afternoon. She entered the lobby, saw Lindsay behind the desk, and strode over when she beckoned. After this morning, Alex couldn't think of her as a kid with braces. Instead, she now saw a young woman who was confident, strong, and passionate.

"Mom texted me," she said. "Dad told her."

"How'd she take it?" Alex asked. "Or could you tell from a text message?"

Lindsay shook her head. "Mom's old school. Believes in full sentences, full paragraphs, even. She's fine. Relieved, actually, to finally know why Dad was being such an idiot. She's also pretty upset he didn't trust her enough to tell her."

"When you hold on to a secret for long enough, it takes on a life of its own."

"Yeah, well, Mr. Langley sure did a number on Dad."

"Do you think he's going to do the right thing?" Alex asked.

"Dad? Absolutely. If he doesn't, he has to deal with both mom and me."

"I wouldn't envy him that!"

Lindsay giggled. "You'd like Mom." The phone rang and she answered. Alex waved to her and headed towards her room.

Alex sat in the wicker lounge on her balcony and watched the waves ripple on the lake. She'd ordered room service again, this time getting a mixed greens salad with mangos, pecans, grilled shrimp, goat cheese, and a cherry vinaigrette. When she'd told Evelyn she wished she could spend all her time on the balcony, she'd meant it. The salad sat on a table to her left and she reached over and speared a piece of mango with her fork. The same young man who'd been setting up the outside bar and who'd brought her breakfast had delivered her lunch.

She sensed nervousness and made small talk. She learned his name was Tommy, and he eventually blurted out that he was concerned about the vote. He needed the job, and if The Mast was sold and converted into a resort, it would be closed down for who knows how long. Plus, he loved working for Ms. Dahl. The roof of his parents' house had been ripped off during the storm, and she let them live at the hotel for a month, asking only that they pay a small incidental fee to help ease the cost of staff and supplies.

It was another example of the kind of person Evelyn was, and what she meant to this community, and what would be lost if Kaine won.

Alex picked up the tablet sitting next to her salad. She'd emailed herself the files from Nick's computer before bringing it to Evelyn's. Something had been tickling her brain since early morning when she'd first read the messages, some inchoate idea. She felt like she was missing something, but what? She opened the email exchange between Nick and Kaine and read, slower this time.

The messages began last November. That must have been when Lars approached Nick for a loan. Nick's subject read "Perfect opportunity." It looked like Kaine ignored him at first, but after the fourth email, he finally answered. *I hate email*, it read. *Call me.*

The man might have hated email, but the back-and-forth continued as their plans developed. It seemed Nick insisted on keeping a written trail, which, as a blackmailer, made sense. Nick told Kaine about the financial straits Lars was in, said he knew Kaine had always wanted to get his hands on The Mast and he should loan him the money. That would give him a foothold.

What about the Reserve? Kaine asked. *That old inn means nothing without the golf course.*

Don't worry. I've got it covered, Nick assured the developer. Which is where, Alex now knew, Phil came in.

As she read the emails from the beginning until the most recent, she began to notice inconsistencies. At times, Kaine's messages were articulate and reasonable. Others, they sounded exactly like he did when he spoke: bombastic, arrogant, dismissive, and demanding. She shoved the salad aside and opened her notebook, jotting thoughts, including the dates and times as well as the subject and overall tone for each exchange.

She'd just finished reading the last one when she heard insistent knocking and looked at the time. Startled to discover it was already quarter after one, she shoved the tablet and her notes into her bag and rushed to her door, bringing the remains of her lunch with her. William stood outside with his hand raised as if to knock again. He grabbed a piece of mango before she put her half-eaten salad on the floor outside her room and they raced down the hall.

"Find something?" he asked as they scrambled down the stairs. Well, she scrambled. William seemed to float effortlessly.

"I think so," she replied, before almost colliding with Ben.

"Whoa there," her ex said, gripping her shoulders to steady her. "I was hoping I'd run into you, but not literally."

"Ben, I don't have time."

"Yes, yes, I know. You're going to the board meeting. As am I. Shall I ride with you?"

"NO," Alex and William said together.

Ben shrugged. "Suit yourself."

The elevator dinged and Harriet walked through the doors. Alex started. She'd forgotten the woman was still here. "There you are," Ben said to her. "I was just suggesting a ride with these two, but they want nothing to do with that."

Harriet smirked. "No, of course they wouldn't. You know how they are. We don't need them, anyway." She looped her arm through Ben's as the two crossed the lobby. He brusquely removed her arm from his and they exited the inn.

"What. Just. Happened?" William asked.

Alex stared after them. "I have no idea," she said, and shook herself off. "C'mon. The county building's half an hour away and we *cannot* be late."

Alex and William arrived at the county government center fifteen minutes before the meeting. They entered the two story building made of Cream City brick and found their way to a large conference room. Outside the open doors, Evelyn stood in the hall talking to a man wearing a blue oxford and gray pleated slacks. They approached the two and Evelyn introduced them. "This is Phil Eliot, our County Board Chairman."

"We've met," Alex smiled warmly, shaking Phil's hand.

"I'm sorry your stay in our county hasn't been as advertised," he said to William.

"That's one way to put it," William said.

Alex elbowed him. "Thank you," she replied to Phil, while searching his face. "I heard things went okay?"

Evelyn looked at her questioningly. Alex shook her head almost imperceptibly.

"Better than I could have hoped. Although apparently Rose, too, thinks I'm an idiot." He looked at his watch. "I've got to get in there. As you undoubtedly know, we've got an important vote this afternoon." He leaned over and kissed Evelyn on the check, and squeezed her hand before turning towards the open door.

At that moment Kaine exploded around the corner, followed closely by Deborah and a man Alex assumed was his attorney. He stopped cold, his eyes narrowing and darting back and forth between Evelyn and Phil. "I knew it," he accused. "You two are in on this together, aren't you? Nick told me you were some kind of tree hugger," he directed at Phil with disdain. "No wonder you delayed the vote yesterday. You've got the hots for this piece, don't you?"

Phil drew his shoulders back, standing to his full height. "Mr. Kaine," he said, "The meeting will begin promptly at two and the doors will be closed at that time. I suggest you and your entourage find a place to sit if you want an opportunity to speak and to be present during the vote." Every bit of the warmth Alex had heard when Phil spoke to Evelyn had been replaced by a stentorian tone. He strode purposefully into the room and down the center aisle towards a table lined with microphones, water pitchers, and glasses beading with condensation. Evelyn, Alex, and William skirted around Kaine, ignoring him completely, and searched for empty seats. Alex swept the room, catching Ben's eyes. He'd chosen a spot in the back row. Harriet sat next to him.

"You're not going to win this," Kaine called after Evelyn. "I own your precious inn. I could own you if I wanted."

Evelyn stiffened, but kept walking. "There we go, right behind Sue," she pointed. They sat down. Evelyn tapped her friend on the shoulder and Sue looked up from the agenda in her hands.

"I see you're going to be speaking. And so will he."

"Yes," Evelyn said as she watched Kaine, Deborah, and the attorney take seats on the other side of the aisle. "Since they detained me yesterday, Phil put us on today."

"Kaine showed up, you know. He was here, right on time. He was supposed to go up after I did," Sue said. As the tourism director, her input on what would happen to the Reserve made sense. "He tried to throw you under the bus, of course," she said to Evelyn.

"Why am I not surprised?"

"He said Nick had been murdered and you were being taken in for questioning. The idiot actually admitted leaving a murder scene and thought the vote would continue, and that it would be in his favor."

William leaned in. "Is it always this dramatic around here?"

Sue laughed and patted his hand. "No, young man, it most certainly is not."

"Well, that's good to know. And thanks for calling me young." He winked. "Now what confuses me is, there's no way this can be kosher. Ms. Nellie Bly over here did some super basic research and even that uncovered the Reserve's importance," he said. "No offense."

"None taken," Alex replied.

"I don't think anyone realized the extent of what Kaine planned until Monday," Sue explained.

"What about the environmental impact study?" William asked. "He had to submit one, right?"

"Oh, he submitted one. Doug, he's the man up there in the flannel shirt, showed it to me this morning." Evelyn spoke to Alex. "It's another unabridged dictionary."

Sue gestured to the thick file sitting in the middle of the table where the board members were gathering. "There's no way they could have read through that entire thing. Especially Tricia."

"Why would she? I tried to talk to her earlier, try to convince her to vote against the course, and she bragged to me about Kaine's rent-free promise," Evelyn explained. "I have a feeling if I offered her the same, she'd be inclined to change her vote."

"Is that an option?" William asked. Alex knew the answer even before Evelyn started shaking her head.

"Absolutely not. I will not be held hostage. Besides, I couldn't afford it even if I were able to keep The Mast."

Phil took his seat at the table and called the meeting to order. Sue turned around to face the front of the room. Alex leaned into Evelyn. "How's Lars?" she whispered.

"His hand will be fine, thank goodness. The hospital had to report it because they could tell it was a gun injury." Evelyn's eyes misted over. "I told Billy it was an accident. I don't know if he believed me, but he can't do anything about it." She spoke softly enough that only Alex could hear her, but the murmuring drew the attention of people around them, so she stopped talking and focused on the seated politicians.

Chapter 19

Phil sat in the middle of a group of five people. To his left were Doug and an impeccably dressed woman Alex assumed was Tricia, the boutique owner. Another man and woman sat on Phil's other side. Alex jiggled her leg until William put his hand on her knee. She believed Phil would do the right thing, but that didn't make her any less anxious. *If she felt like this, how must Evelyn be feeling?* she wondered.

Phil called Evelyn and she stood up, sidled around Alex and William, and approached the microphone. She cleared her throat and spoke clearly. "Good afternoon, everyone. Thank you for the opportunity to speak with you.

"As you know, as I'm sure everyone in this room knows considering what an intimate community we are, two days ago I signed a contract to sell The Mast. It was the toughest decision I've ever had to make, but I did it because I felt like I had no choice. I thought it was the only way to save what my great-great-grandfather began more than a century ago when he founded Alvin's Landing."

"Nice touch," William whispered. "Way to pull at those heart strings." Alex put her finger to her lips.

"I knew the buyer would want to make changes, of course. The Mast has been around for just a little while." Light chuckles floated around the room. "However, I did not know how drastic those changes would be."

Kaine jumped up and flung his hand towards Evelyn. He was so close to her he nearly hit her. "What's going on here? I thought this was supposed to be about the Reserve vote, not her stupid hotel," he yelled.

"Mr. Kaine, you will have your time to speak," Phil said. "Please refrain from interrupting Ms. Dahl, and I'm sure she'll give you the same consideration."

Evelyn pulled her eyes from Kaine and dipped her head to acknowledge the board chair. "Thank you, Mr. Eliot. The most drastic of those changes," she continued, "is the conversion of the Alvin's Landing Nature Reserve into an eighteen-hole golf course. I realize this was announced several weeks ago. What I did not realize was the extent of the destruction and the irreparable damage the course would do." She paused. "I mistakenly believed that the impact would be minimal, based on the initial reports Mr. Kaine submitted."

Alex realized Evelyn refused to put the blame for the situation that had necessitated the sale on her brother, even though he'd been the primary liaison with Kaine.

She would not let anyone know Lars had reviewed the reports and then provided a summary to his sister, leaving out pertinent information, like the fact that holes 3, 7, and 13 would replace the Reserve's unique ecosystems.

"I'm the first to admit that I've been against this from the start, but I'll also admit my initial opposition was almost purely emotional."

"Ha! Big surprise there."

"Mr. Kaine!" Phil clipped. "One more interruption and I will bar you from these proceedings."

Evelyn continued, her voice steady. "Almost everyone in this room either grew up with that Reserve or spent summer visits exploring it. How many hikes and picnics have we had there?" She turned to the man on the opposite side of the table from Doug. "Kevin, I remember when you proposed to Mary on the overlook. I think you gave Nick the idea." She swallowed before continuing. "The Grove Shelter is where we've celebrated birthdays, anniversaries, graduations. That whole Reserve is a piece of us. It's part of our story.

"But we also have to accept that sometimes change is necessary for growth. Nick," she stopped as her voice caught, "Nick pointed out to me that things were stagnant and they needed to change. He was right; they do.

"Not like this, though, not by destroying someplace magical. Not by taking away something that all of us—" she turned her head around the room and made eye contact with several people. Alex recognized faces from the last two days: Joy from the diner, and Brenda, the bartender at Rowdy Cormorant, and Georgia and her entire band. They all acknowledged the petite redhead's impassioned plea. "—all of us can enjoy, and replacing it with something that only a very few will ever use.

"I acknowledge I will definitively lose The Mast if you vote to allow Mr. Kaine to build his golf course. That's fine." Evelyn shrugged and laughed softly. "Well, it's not fine, but it's what's going to happen. I've already signed the paperwork."

"And you get a few million out of it, don't you?" the impeccably dressed woman said, leaning into her microphone.

Phil glared at her. "Mrs. Overton, please let Ms. Dahl finish or we will once again table this vote."

"Yes, I will, Tricia," Evelyn acknowledged. "I'll get several million, in fact, even after paying back taxes." She looked down at her clasped hands. "I could tell you that money doesn't matter to me, but that wouldn't be entirely true. Would it be nice to never have to worry again? Absolutely. But at what cost?"

She looked at each of the board members. "As Mr. Kaine rightly pointed out, this meeting is about the Reserve. It's not about The Mast, and it's not about me. It is, however, about Alvin's Landing, and the kind of place you want to live. That Reserve is as much a part of this peninsula as the marinas, the lighthouses, and the cherry orchards. There's a reason we have so many parks; we value our natural wonders.

"If Mr. Kaine builds that golf course, if you vote to turn our park over to a developer, not only will we lose a piece of our past, but we'll also lose three unique ecosystems. Unique, as in, they are nowhere else on earth.

"For what? A 'good walk spoiled'?" She lifted her chin a little higher, straightened up a little more. "It will be a good deal more than a walk that's spoiled. As a business owner—"

"Former," Kaine coughed.

"—a descendant of Alvin Dahl himself, who founded the village and the Reserve, and your friend, I beg you to do the right thing for our community. Please vote no. Please save Alvin's Landing." Evelyn tipped her head to the board and made her way back to her seat.

Sue turned around and gripped Evelyn's hand and smiled. "Good job," she mouthed.

On the other side of the aisle, Kaine stood up. Deborah put his briefcase on his chair and opened it towards her. He clapped slowly, glaring at Evelyn as he stepped to the microphone.

"Very nice," he said. "Very dramatic." His eyes swept the room. "She's right about one thing: this is about your community, and the kind of place you want to live. Do you want progress to pass you by? Do you want to be broke? Do you want to always have to scramble for jobs? For money? A park is nice. But a park won't pay the bills.

"Tourism drives this county. Always has. Always will. Sure, the park will draw your tree huggers, your outdoor enthusiasts, whatever you call them. But here's the thing. You've already got tons of parks in this county. How many state parks? How many county parks? There's even a National Wildlife Refuge. I mean, really, how many parks does one county need? You're seriously not going to miss one, especially when it's not even one of your bigger parks. It's one of the smallest in the county.

"You know what people who so love the outdoors don't do?" He waved his hands, mocking those nature-loving tourists. "They don't spend money. They hike, for free. They hunt and fish, for free. They ride their bikes, or have a 'picnic'" Kaine sneered, "or look at the view from pretty overlooks."

Several people gasped. That was cold, even for Kaine, Alex thought.

Kevin, the man at the end of the table, interjected. "We require permits for both fishing and hunting, and charge fees for those."

Kaine scoffed. "What? A few bucks a year? How much do you make on that? I bet it wouldn't even buy you a week's worth of bait.

"That Reserve is a gold mine. Or it could be. It *will* be, once I get a hold of it." His eyes glowed with greed. "We'll turn it into the best golf course in the country, connected to the best resort and spa in the country, with the best restaurant. We'll turn that dive Rowdy Cormorant into a Michelin-starred destination." Georgia and her band booed until Phil's glare quieted them. "Alvin's Landing will be a destination—for the wealthy. For the rich. And they're going to spend their money here, with you. They'll buy your clothes," he pointed to Tricia. "They'll tee off on the greens you design and maintain," he jabbed at Doug. He turned towards Sue. "Can you picture your new Visitors Guide? It'll be a catalog, the type of catalog people like me buy from."

The doors opened and heads craned to see who made the disturbance. Billy entered. Kaine glared. "Continue, please," Billy motioned. "Sorry to interrupt." He closed the doors behind him and leaned against the wall, crossing his arms.

"YMC-hey you can arrest me," William whispered to Alex.

She stifled a chuckle. "Stop, you. This is not the time to be joking."

"I think it's precisely the time to be joking. As in, that man," he said, pointing to Kaine, "is a joke. Like anyone's going to want people like him to come here."

"That's where you're mistaken, my friend. Just look at Tricia and Doug. If there were buzzers to vote 'Yes' they'd have slammed them by now."

"Excuse me," Kaine directed towards them. "May I continue?"

William looked around. "You're talking to us? Oh, sure. I do love a good story." This time it was Evelyn's turn to smother a laugh.

Kaine narrowed his eyes, but then turned back towards the board. "As I was saying, I will bring money to this county." He put his hand out. Deborah pulled a sheath of papers from the briefcase and handed them to him. He flourished it for dramatic effect. "This is the contract for The Mast. This is the contract for your future. It is up to you whether it's the same broken-down town you've always had, or if it becomes a place where people like me actually want to visit."

"He honestly thinks that's a selling point?" William asked under his breath. Sue didn't turn around, but she gave him a thumbs up.

"If you vote no, you're voting to stay in the past," Kaine continued. "Vote yes, and you vote for wealth. You vote for prosperity. You vote for the future."

He walked the couple of feet to his seat and handed the papers back to Deborah. She put them in the briefcase, shut it, and set it on the floor in front of his chair as he sat down.

A low buzzing interrupted the silence. Heads craned to see where the noise originated. Alex saw Billy, still by the doors, holding his phone in front of him. Kaine looked around, the same as everyone else, then tilted his head towards his feet. He bent down and picked up his briefcase. He opened it and pulled out a phone, the screen lit up by an incoming call. He answered. "Hello?

Who the hell is this?" His voice echoed from the phone in the detective's hand.

Chapter 20

Billy ended the call and Kaine pulled the phone away from his ear, staring at the screen with a look of confusion on his face. Alex watched as he reached into his suit coat pocket and pulled out another device. From where she sat, it looked like the same model as the one in his hand. He turned to Deborah. She leaned over and whispered something in her boss's ear; he put the phone back in the briefcase, shut it, and shoved it in front of his assistant with his foot.

Phil cleared his throat and spoke. "The board will now adjourn for a brief deliberation. When we return, we will announce the results of the vote." The board collectively stood up and walked towards a door in the room's corner. Conversations broke the silence.

"You told Billy about the text messages, I'm guessing," Alex murmured to William.

"I sure did. Nick's cell is nowhere to be found and his provider just released the records, so Billy hadn't seen the texts yet. I gave him a heads up and even advised him to look for a certain number." William turned around and grinned at the detective, following him with his eyes as Billy moved to the side of the room. "Billy said there was one time and place he knew for sure where Kaine would be, so here he is."

Alex lightly kissed his cheek. "You're a doll, although I can't believe you didn't tell me."

"You've got your secrets; I've got mine," he winked. "That'll teach you."

Evelyn leaned towards the two. "Does this mean what I think it means?" When Alex nodded, she continued. "I wonder why he's not arresting him?"

"Doesn't have enough evidence yet, I bet. They're waiting on the ballistics report," William answered.

Alex appraised her friend. "Huh," she said.

"What?" he asked, the picture of innocence.

"Sounds like you two had some conversation." She turned to watch Kaine, who'd stalked to the front of the room, followed by his assistant and attorney. She couldn't hear what they were saying over the din of voices, but there was lots of hand waving going on. "I think he knows his goose is well and thoroughly cooked," she said.

The door in the corner opened and the board filed back in. "That was fast," Evelyn said. Sue reached back and squeezed her friend's hand.

Phil pulled the microphone towards him and called the room to order. Deborah and the attorney returned to their seats, but Kaine stood near the front of the room, his arms crossed. Alex noticed Doug and Tricia refused to look at him.

"As Chair of the County Supervisory Board, it is my solemn duty, it is *our* duty," Phil gestured to his fellow board members, "to do what is best for this county. Our concerns are not just about the economic health of this region, but also about our residents' quality of life."

He paused and looked directly at Evelyn as he spoke. "That makes it my distinct pleasure to announce that the board has voted unanimously to oppose Mr. Kaine's motion to turn Alvin's Landing Nature Reserve into a golf course."

"WHAT?!" Kaine roared. He leapt towards the table, but before he reached it, Billy raced around in front of him, blocking his path.

"I don't think you want to do what you were just about to do," Billy said, putting his hand on Kaine's chest to stop him from getting any closer to the board members. "I advise you to calm down, sir, or I will have to take you into custody."

Kaine's head whipped back and forth. He jabbed his finger in the air, pointing at Doug, at Tricia, at Phil. "You're going to regret this. I know about you. I know all about you." His head swiveled to the crowd who watched him, rapt. He pointed at Doug and Tricia. "You know what those two have going on? I'll tell you. Each other, that's what. They've been having an affair for years. Nick told me all about it."

"Tell us something we don't know," Joy shouted, her hand cupped around the side of her mouth. The room laughed.

"Yeah, you fool. Everybody in this room knows about their 'secret' romance," Georgia continued. When Doug and Tricia turned towards her in surprise, she continued. "It's about time it was out in the open. You two haven't been fooling anyone."

Phil tapped a gavel. "Mr. Kaine—"

"And YOU," Kaine shouted. "I know all about you, too. Nick filled me in on your so-called alibi." He pointed at Phil. "He's the one you need to take in for questioning."

Billy looked at Phil, who nodded and spoke. "He already knows, Mr. Kaine. He knows everything."

Kaine sputtered. "But I had you! I had the vote! That Reserve is mine!"

Phil stood up to his full height. "According to the vote made by this duly elected board, Mr. Kaine, it is not. It would seem that, in your words, we're all tree huggers."

Kaine visibly reined himself in. He pulled back his shoulders and slowly turned his head towards Evelyn. A wicked smile contorted his features. "Fine. You know what I do have? Your precious Mast. I'm going to raze it to the ground and leave it there, a festering hole. No more marina, no more Rowdy Cormorant, no more grandpa's legacy, or whatever sentimental crap you call it." He scanned the room with flared nostrils, a look of pure evil on his face. "And there's nothing you can do about it."

He strode down the center aisle, knocking the microphone stand over as he passed. Deborah got up slowly, straightened her skirt, and followed him out, the attorney scrambling behind her.

The packed room sat in stunned silence in the wake of a grown man's tantrum. After a few moments, Evelyn rose from her chair and crossed to the microphone stand, stood it back upright, and walked to the front of the room. She turned to face everyone, taking a deep breath before smiling gently.

"Well, you heard the man," she said. "The Reserve is saved!" Cheers erupted.

"But what about The Mast?" a man sitting next to Joy asked when everyone had quieted.

Evelyn inhaled, stood up straighter, and looked around the room at all the faces, all these people she knew, and Alex felt their love for this small, fierce fighter. "What Mr. Kaine does with it is out of my hands now. But, as Tricia pointed out, I'll be making a pretty penny on this sale, so who knows what I will do? This is my home; Alvin's Landing is my home. You are my neighbors and always will be. No matter what, I will stay here, and even Kaine destroys The Mast, its spirit will live on. This, I promise you."

William whispered to Alex. "That woman needs to run for office."

"Since it sounds like this is our last hurrah," Evelyn said, "and since the most important thing—the Reserve—is saved, how would you all feel about a little celebration?" She looked at her watch. "Our Chicago duo will be setting up in the gazebo soon and it's a gorgeous day. Would you like to join me for some live music and adult beverages? I know I could certainly use one or two." Friends and neighbors quickly surrounded Evelyn, wanting to shake her hand, or hug her, or both. Phil made eye contact with Alex and gave her a small smile before walking over to Billy. William's eyes focused on the detective, which by now didn't surprise Alex in the slightest. She'd seen her friend have crushes before, but it seemed like this one might be a little more serious. It might even be reciprocated, she thought, as she watched the officer give her friend his own secret smile before turning to Phil.

William finally broke his gaze and glanced at Alex. "What's going on in that head of yours? I can hear your synapses firing. It's like a disco ball in there, isn't it?"

"I'm still wondering if it's possible to save The Mast."

"Of course you are. What are you thinking?"

"If Kaine's arrested, he can't exactly buy it, now can he?"

"And he still hasn't deposited the funds in the escrow account," Sue said. "Although he has until tomorrow." She stood up. "I need to call Juke and fill him in."

"Where is Mr. Tall Dark and Dreamy?" William asked.

"He had a lunch charter, but he should be back by now." She excused herself and walked towards the side of the room, holding her phone to her ear. Several people tried to stop and talk to her, but she put them off with a smile and a raised finger. She hung up and made her way back.

"You know, it seems like he's much more Evelyn's type than Nick was." Alex said when Sue returned.

"What, Juke? Oh, he's definitely more her type. Star-crossed lovers. Maybe now..." Sue shook that idea from her head. "I don't want to get my hopes up."

They joined the crowd spilling out into the hallway. The three waited as Evelyn stopped several times on her way towards them, accepting more handshakes and hugs. It was an odd atmosphere. A man had been murdered and a few favorite businesses were about to be destroyed, but the Reserve had been saved. It felt like everyone was breathing a constrained sigh of relief, and it seemed to Alex that anyone who'd been in favor of Kaine's plans had been in a distinct minority. Even Doug and Tricia changed their votes. The board must have had a pretty convincing discussion, Alex thought.

And yet, those plans had gotten to the point where, if Nick hadn't been killed, Kaine would have gotten his way. It's amazing what a little blackmail and bribery, and a lot of greed, could do. Alex wondered yet again why Kaine murdered his goose before he knew it would lay the golden egg.

Alex and William clinked their plastic cups together. "Cheers!"

"I think this is the best Old Fashioned yet," William said after tasting the cocktail. "To whom do we owe the pleasure?" he asked the young man bartending. It was

Tommy, the same young man Alex had seen multiple times stocking this very bar, delivering her breakfast and lunch, and now bartending.

"Thank you, sir. My name's Tommy. Oh, hi Mom," he said, as Sue reached the bar. He turned around and pulled a pint from a tap labeled Bridge Up. Sue took the beer from him and moved aside for the next person in line.

"This lovely young man is your son?" Alex asked as she watched him expertly mix another cocktail.

"He sure is. Been working here every summer since he was sixteen." Sue leaned over and whispered dramatically. "Evelyn is his hero." She winked at her son and then motioned William and Alex away from the bar towards the marina. Everyone who'd been at the vote was there, milling about on the grass, kicking their shoes off to walk on the sand, and relaxing on the Adirondack chairs. If one didn't know better, it would seem like a typical summer celebration.

"He told me about your roof during last fall's storm," Alex said.

Sue put her hand on her heart. "What a nightmare. If Evelyn hadn't helped, I don't know what we would have done. She's my closest friend, but she helped anyone who needed it," she said as they walked past the gazebo, where a woman tuned her guitar and a man organized the cables leading to their sound system. Alex smiled to herself, realizing this was the singer-songwriter duo from Chicago that Tommy had mentioned to her on her first day. She didn't think she'd be able to see them, and now here she was.

Her smile disappeared as she considered why. This was a celebration, of sorts, and as Alex looked at the forest behind the fishing shack and Brannigan's Charters, she felt gratitude that the Reserve would survive. But that fishing shack would be gone, and so would Juke's building. Her eyes swept the entire complex, from the Rowdy Cormorant to the edge of the inn and her corner balcony and back to the gazebo. How quickly would Kaine demolish it, she wondered, because she knew he would make good on his threat.

"Earth to Alex," William waved, and then followed her eyes. "Ah. I see. I'd be staring, too. In fact, I think I'll join you in appreciating that fine example of the human species."

"What?" Alex cleared her head. "Staring at what?" Her eyes focused on the man adjusting the height of the microphone stand, and she smiled. "I know you won't believe me, but I didn't even notice him. Speaking of noticing, there's Detective Pierce." She pointed her drink towards the officer walking towards them. Alvin, the cat, followed close on his heels.

"I take it my tip paid off, Detective Pierce," William grinned. "I'm surprised to see you here, although I'm not complaining."

Sue glanced from one to the other and smirked. Billy reached down to pick up Alvin before responding. "I'm getting a certain computer from Evelyn," he said, while looking at Alex.

She ignored his comment, reaching over to scratch behind Alvin's ear. The cat began purring. She could feel Billy's eyes on her, but she thought it better to stay quiet. William jumped in. "Is it Nick's?" he asked, all bright eyed and innocent.

Billy rolled his eyes and put the cat down. He turned around and walked towards Evelyn, but they all noticed that he didn't seem particularly upset and there even seemed to be a little swagger in his step.

"Well, I'll be. It's about darned time," Sue said.

Alex pulled her eyes away from her lovesick friend to focus on the woman next to her. "You said Kaine hadn't deposited the money in the escrow account," she said, with no preamble.

"Evelyn told me last night, and as of the meeting, he still hadn't sent it. She's holding onto a sliver of hope. I think that's the only thing keeping her going."

"That, and possibly him," Alex said, as she watched Juke reach Evelyn. He pulled her into a hug, but after they released she walked away, leaving him standing alone. "Or maybe not."

"Poor Juke," Sue said. "He just needs to give her time." She took a drink and wiped a bit of foam from her upper lip. "Feels odd, doesn't it? A celebration that really isn't." Alex agreed. "I'm afraid this might seem rather insensitive, but I need to put on my tourism director hat for a moment, if you'll forgive me. Do you think you two will write about Alvin's Landing?" Alex could hear the concern in her voice. What could two travel writers possibly say after the visit they'd had?

"Yes," William said, unequivocally. "I've got an assignment to cover the Reserve and the other parks in the county." Sue visibly relaxed.

"And I've got a few ideas brewing," Alex assured her. "I'll be here through the end of the week. Why don't we talk tomorrow?"

"Sounds good," Sue agreed, then continued sadly. "I apologize for bringing it up, but I need to salvage something from this week, if I can. Our board doesn't have the biggest budget." Sue paused. "Well, I'm going to make some rounds. I'll email you."

Alex watched Sue walk towards a cluster of people, who smiled, and hugged, and clapped her on the back, and shook hands, and did all the hearty bonhomie things people do when they're at a party. But it was stilted, forced, with an undercurrent of sorrow. The guitarist picked out a minor chord. The singer introduced the duo, then they began a haunting sea shanty. His rich voice resonated, the backdrop of the inn creating a reverberation. Conversations silenced, and even the servers passing canapes stopped and listened. Alex stood, enchanted. It was a mournful song that seemed to articulate the emotional undercurrent.

Her phone buzzed, breaking the spell. Ben.

Chapter 21

Alex had a short drive because her destination was near the tip of the peninsula where it narrowed. Along the way, she thought through everything she knew about what had occurred in the past few days. She reviewed her certainty that Kaine killed Nick, admonishing herself; she'd considered no one else, not really, and she knew their previous experience influenced her focus on him. Her old editors had always warned Alex to report objectively, and while she kept her emotions out of her stories, she hated it. The necessity for objectivity was one reason she'd found another medium that allowed her to write for a living, one where she could express her convictions.

Alex pulled into a parking lot across the street from a sparkling bay, an evergreen-crowned island in the distance. The lot provided overflow space for a restaurant housed inside a two-story neoclassical mansion with white siding and Doric columns flanking the massive front porch. Alex turned off the ignition and watched a valet sneak around the corner of the house and light a cigarette, then she got out and walked over to a black and chrome Hummer. She motioned for Ben to roll down his window.

"Is she still in there?"

"Hello to you, too," Ben replied. "She hasn't come out yet, not that I've seen."

"And him?"

"No sign of him, but the bartender texted me she moved to a corner booth, so I bet he's on his way."

"They've been here every night," Ben answered her unspoken question. "I tip the bartender really, really well, and he returns the favor. So to speak."

"Thanks for letting me know," Alex said. "I appreciate it." She paused, wanting to say more, but knowing she needed to get inside. She knew he didn't have to fill her in, and his relentless optimism that they'd get back together was sometimes flattering. Right now, it even made her miss him a bit. That was, until she remembered Ben's 'optimism' was actually, as William called it, stalking her. She knew she had to somehow make it crystal clear that they were done, forever, although that would be hard to do if she kept using his assistance. What was at stake was worth more than a minor inconvenience, she thought. But once this was over, she was going to set Ben straight.

The golden hour neared and Alex looked across the bay. The island was in shadow and she shielded her eyes from the sun, its reflection glinting on the water like gold coins. She mounted the steps and pulled back a heavy ten-foot tall door that creaked with age. Once inside, Alex's eyes took a moment to adjust, and she saw the blonde sitting in a semi-circular booth in the corner, where Ben said she'd be. Alex noted the blonde was the only person in the place who wasn't paid to be there. The two women made eye contact. Alex strode towards her and sat down without asking. A young man with carefully tousled black hair and pristine skin approached the table. Alex pointed at the woman's half-empty martini glass, a plastic pick speared through a single green olive resting on its rim. "I'll have the same," she ordered.

Deborah picked up her drink, the bottom half of the angled glass still frosted, and appraised her over the rim. "I wondered."

"When I'd make the connection?"

"I told you I knew who killed Nick. You didn't seem to take me seriously."

The server approached with a martini shaker and a chilled glass containing three bleu-cheese stuffed olives. He shook the silver bullet-shaped receptacle in an elaborate figure eight motion, his hair flipping with each change of direction, before pouring the vodka in a long stream. Alex took a sip of the murky liquid, not surprised it was dirty. She toyed with the spear of olives, considering how she could get the information she needed.

Before she could say anything, the front door slammed open and Kaine entered. He saw the two women and strode towards them. He stopped next to where Deborah sat facing the room. "Move."

His assistant held his gaze, her eyes flashing for one brief moment. She scooted towards the direct center of the booth until she sat equidistant between Kaine and Alex. The young man hurried over with a three-finger pour of brown liquor and left just as quickly.

Kaine looked from one woman to the other. "What's going on here?"

"You mean you don't know, Trevor?" Deborah asked, running her finger around the rim of her glass. "I thought you knew everything."

He reared back, startled. Clearly, she'd never challenged him before. He recovered quickly, reaching into his left pocket, pulling out a phone and placing it on the table. Then he reached into his right pocket and extracted another phone, the same model with the same case, and set it next to the other. He tapped the one on his left. "Guess what's on this phone, Debbie?" He leaned in, pushing the table forward.

"It's Deborah, Trevor. My name is Deborah."

"A text message to Nick?" Alex ventured.

Kaine whipped his head towards her, but Deborah focused on her drink and slowly smiled. "I told you she was smart, Trevor, but you never listen to me, do you?" She looked up and took a bite of her last olive. "Oh, you listen to me sometimes, but only when I'm saying what you want to hear."

"How dare you," he sputtered.

"How dare I?" Deborah continued, unperturbed. "I've been daring for a very long time. You just never noticed."

"I made you. I'm the reason for all of this," he said, gesturing towards her chest, her face, her hair.

"You're definitely responsible, but you are in no way, shape, or form the reason, Trevor. That honor falls to Nick," Deborah said. Alex drew in air with a low whistle, and the blonde peered at her as she finished the olive. "She knows. Don't you, Alex?"

The disco ball, as William had so descriptively called her brain, was in full swing. She pointed to the phone near Kaine's left hand. "That's the phone you use to conduct business for him."

"Very good."

"And you sent the text to Nick for the meeting on the overlook," Alex continued.

Deborah's lips curled, a serpentine curve. Kaine picked up his glass and stopped mid-air. "It was you? You killed Nick?" He set his drink back down and his eyes narrowed in disbelief, and Alex could see the realization cross his face. It was practically a light bulb over his head. "You're the reason we lost the Reserve? You couldn't have waited until after the vote? This is *your* fault?" His volume increased with the level of his incredulity, with his anger - not that she had killed Nick, but that her timing sucked.

He started to stand. Deborah stopped him. "I wouldn't do that, if I were you," she said coldly, her eyes roaming carefully around the room, confirming the bartender and server were focused on their phones and weren't paying attention to the drama playing out in the corner booth. She reached into her giant Louis Vuitton bag and pulled out a pistol, displaying it long enough for them both to see and then she put her hand, and the gun, back under the table.

Alex held her breath. Kaine still didn't get it, she realized. He didn't know why Debbie —Deborah—had done it. She was the woman nobody paid attention to, and then when she transformed herself, it was into such a caricature that no one paid attention to her then either, including the man she'd devoted her life to or the man who'd inspired her transformation. She was one of Trevor Kaine's appendages, nothing more, and neither he nor Nick had taken her seriously.

Alex was taking her seriously now. She wondered if Kaine would, too, before it was too late.

"I know neither one of you cares if the other is shot, but neither one of you knows at whom I'm pointing right now, do you?" She raised her other arm to get the server's attention. "Mr. Kaine will pay the tab now," she said. "We're going to call it an early night."

Kaine pulled out his wallet and put a black American Express on the table, never taking his eyes off his assistant. "You'll regret this."

Deborah threw her head back, laughing, then leveled her black eyes at her boss. "You are such a cliché. Isn't he a cliché? I'm looking forward to finally being done with you and your trite lines and your limited vocabulary and your unlimited arrogance. How you ever got this far, I'll never know. Oh wait, I do know." She stopped. "Because of me. You owe everything to me. And I'm going to take what's mine."

It was Alex's turn to laugh; it was purely reflex. "Talk about a cliché," she muttered, then picked up her martini.

"Yes, laugh, Alex, laugh. You should get as much enjoyment as possible in the little time you have left."

Alex couldn't help herself. She guffawed, spitting out her vodka and spraying Kaine's phones. The situation was ludicrous. A gun had been pointed in her general direction twice in two days and here she was stuck with two villains straight from central casting: the greedy chump and the femme fatale.

Kaine snatched a napkin and unrolled it, scattering the silverware across the table, and wiped off the screens. "Just what do you plan to do, Debbie?"

"It is Deborah," she said. "It has always been Deborah, and you will afford me some respect for once in our miserable time together. I have a gun pointed at you, and I will use it."

"You'll be caught," he said.

"And you'll be dead." Deborah finished the last sip of vodka, swallowing the liquor and bits of bleu cheese that had sunk to the bottom of the glass. "We'll just wait until the server returns with your card, shall we? Then we're going to take a little drive. And don't-"

"Oh oh, let me. Can I finish? 'And don't even think of doing anything stupid.' That's what you were going to say, right?" Alex was nearly hysterical. She survived cancer. She didn't want to die because of some obviously unbalanced psychopath. Maybe Evelyn was right and she should have left this all in Billy's hands.

The server returned the folio. Kaine extracted his card and put it back in his wallet, and Deborah motioned them out of the booth. Kaine got up first and walked stiffly to the front door, followed closely by Alex. He turned his head to the bar. "Don't," Deborah said. They filed out of the mansion and Alex looked into the overflow lot. Ben's Hummer was gone. The valet was nowhere to be seen. They walked along the side of the house towards the back. Alex crossed her arms over her chest, uncrossed them, and put her hands in her pants pockets.

"Keep your hands visible, Ms. Paige." She'd parked the pearl Lexus next to a battered green dumpster, an incongruous sight. Deborah told Alex to open both passenger side doors, then motioned for Kaine to sit in the back and scoot to the far side. She instructed Alex to get in the driver's seat, keeping her gun-toting designer bag trained on one, then the other, going back and forth.

"Buckle up," she said. Alex complied, and then Deborah closed the front passenger side door and joined Kaine in the back seat. "Now drive."

"You can't do this!" Kaine yelled. "Debbie—Deborah—listen to me. Look, I'll give you anything you want."

"You can't give me what I want." She pulled the gun out of her bag and pointed it at Alex's head. "Drive."

"Where are you taking us?" Kaine asked.

"She's smart. She knows where to go. Right, Ms. Paige?"

Alex nodded as she pulled around the dumpster, frantically searching for Ben's giant black and chrome vehicle. *Of all the times for him to not be a stalker*, she thought.

Chapter 22

The sun slipped below the tree line. Alex kept her eyes forward as she drove the exact speed limit, terrified to even look in the mirrors. She turned into the Reserve and the car's headlights lit up the sign. Someone had crossed out *Save our home. Say NO to Kaine's course!* and written *WE DID!* in thick black marker. Kaine saw the sign and cursed. "Fools," he said. "They're all fools."

"They are not fools," Alex said with scorn. "They simply place value on things you'll never understand."

"She's right about that," Deborah spoke up. "They seem to believe in loyalty. A concept that's beyond your grasp."

Alex pulled into the small parking area at the base of the overlook and turned off the ignition. Someone had replaced the caution tape. She dared to glimpse into the rearview mirror and made eye contact with Deborah. "Why?" she asked.

Deborah reached behind her back and pulled the handle, pushing the door open with her elbow. She waved the gun at them. "You want the grand finale where all is revealed? Fine. We'll walk and talk. Get out and start climbing." Deborah backed out of the car, training the gun on them the entire time as they followed her directions. Kaine ripped the caution tape off and mounted the stairs. Alex followed him, and Deborah delivered her monologue as they crossed one landing, then another, getting ever closer to the top.

"It's simple, really. I wanted Nick. Had wanted him since he first approached you after you were released from prison, Trevor. I thought, a man like that, who sees someone nobody else will touch and thinks it's an opportunity? Now that's a man.

"Not like you," she said to Kaine's back with contempt. "You always take the easy way out. The sure thing."

"He didn't this time," Alex paused, then flinched when Deborah pressed the gun into her back.

"Keep moving. You don't think so? Nick did all the work. *He's* the one who lined up the sale. *He* brought Lars to you on a silver platter, didn't he, Trevor?"

Kaine reached the top landing and turned to look down at Alex and Deborah. "But Nick needed me to make it happen, now didn't he?" he snapped. "He came begging me. 'Please oh please buy this inn,'" he mocked. "Practically got on his knees."

Deborah pulled the gun from Alex's back and pointed it at Kaine. "Do not push me, Trevor." Kaine shut up as Deborah motioned the weapon toward the benches. "Sit next to each other. Cozy. Like you like each other.

CLOSER. Now sit on your hands." They did as directed. Alex felt the skin on her arm recoil as it touched Kaine's sleeve. From this altitude, she could still see the sun as it set to the west. She squinted, unable to see Deborah's features. Alex lifted her hand to shield her eyes, but Deborah waved the gun. "Uh-uh-uh," she sang. "Put that hand back where it belongs."

Deborah cackled. "Now who's a cliché? I am. I'm a cliché. The grand villain tells all before doing away with her nemeses. It's rather magnificent, isn't it? The view of the lake with a beautiful Midwestern setting sun, and here I am with the power to end both of your lives and there's nothing you can do about it.

"Now where was I? Oh yes. Nick gave you Lars, Trevor, which gave you The Mast. He gave you the board, too. He knew how to make people do things. He knew how to get what he wanted. He deserved better than Evelyn, that insipid goody-two-shoes," she spat.

Alex flashed to Deborah sitting in the lounge's corner, watching as Evelyn placed her engagement ring in Nick's hand, as she slapped him, and she remembered Deborah smiling. It hadn't registered until now.

"I see you understand," Deborah said. "Go ahead. Why don't you fill Mr. Kaine in? Because he's obviously clueless." She walked over to stand in front of the far railing and her eyes bore into his, the sun no longer blinding them.

Alex looked at Deborah's smug face. She was so proud of herself, so pleased with her manipulations and plans. "Are you sure you don't want the honor?"

Deborah kept her eyes on Kaine's, and Alex knew she'd moved so she'd no longer be backlit and he could see the triumph on her face. How long she must have harbored the hatred emanating from her every pore. "No. I want him to realize how stupid he truly is, and that he's once again outwitted by a woman. Please, continue," she said, waving the gun like a baton.

"You saw Evelyn break up with Nick and followed him," Alex started. "You tried to console him, right? Tried to convince him he didn't need her, that he was better off without her."

"And he was."

"You offered yourself in her place, but he wanted nothing to do with you, did he? He thought you were plastic, fake, and nobody like you could ever replace his Evelyn, a natural beauty, a kind person, someone everyone loved." Alex knew she was pushing the other woman. She wanted to make her so angry she'd do something irrational. Isn't that what happened in all the novels?

Deborah appraised her and ignored her taunts. "It won't work. Continue the story. Now."

Alex swallowed and looked away from Deborah and the lake to the other corner of the overlook. She looked down, through the open air, and snapped her eyes back to the gun. "He rejected you and you were furious. How dare he? After everything you'd done for him. Because this," and with that Alex moved her head up and down to indicate Deborah's body, "transformation was all for him, wasn't it?"

"I told you she was smart, Trevor. Keep going."

"Then he brushed you off, told you he wanted nothing to do with you," Alex watched Deborah's grip on the gun tighten and she knew she was getting to her; just a little longer. "That was the last straw; after years of being Kaine's lap dog, you'd had enough of men ignoring you and pushing you aside. You'd show Nick; you'd show everyone. You sent Nick a text from Kaine's phone, the one you keep and use to manage his business. He never touches that phone, does he?"

"We covered that already, but if I could put this gun down, I'd clap."

"Nick met you up here," Alex continued. "I'm guessing he was surprised to see you. You gave him one more chance to accept your offer, accept you, and when he rejected you, again, you killed him." Out of the corner of her eye, she could see Kaine's eyes widen as he began to understand.

"He had two opportunities to accept this," Deborah said, smoothing her free hand down her hip. "He made the wrong choice."

"You killed Nick, then took his phone, and while we were on the tour, you pretended to call him, but really you used his phone to text Evelyn. You texted Nick the night before from Kaine's phone to get him up here, and sent the text to Evelyn to make it look like Kaine was framing her.

"Diabolical," Alex finished.

"I prefer the word brilliant."

"Ha!" Kaine interrupted. "Hardly brilliant if she figured it all out."

"Do you really want to antagonize me right now, Trevor?" Deborah motioned for Alex to keep going. "You've come this far. Now tell us, what do I plan to do now?"

Alex refused to answer. Deborah walked over and put the tip of the gun under her chin. "You're doing so well, Ms. Paige. Do continue." She glared at Kaine while speaking to Alex: "I want to hear from your mouth how brilliant I am."

Just a little more time, Alex thought. She needed a little more time. "Fine, fine, can you please back up? Please. I'm begging you," her voice broke, and she began crying. Why had it taken her so long to start crying? Shock, she decided. She was in shock. Alex gulped. "You're going to shoot Kaine, then you're going to make me help you throw his body over the railing, and then you'll push me off. You'll wipe the gun and place it near my hand, making it look like I shot him and we fought and fell over the railing together."

Deborah laughed with glee. "Oh, you are good!" She sobered and pointed the gun at Kaine. "Now get up, both of you."

They obeyed. "You're never going to get away with this," Kaine growled.

"Blah blah blah. Don't you ever tire of being such a bloviated, predictable pig? I know the answer to that—no, you don't, and I simply cannot abide one more minute with you on this earth."

Alex jumped to the side and fell on the slats as Billy leapt over the top stair and tackled Deborah. She fell forward. A shot fired. Alex scooted towards the other side of the landing as Officer Hampton scrambled by her. Kaine covered his abdomen with his hands. He pulled them away, stared at the blood, shocked, then began falling backward, backward, into the railing. Alex watched in horror as the upper beam pulled away from the corner post and he disappeared over the edge.

Billy yanked Deborah up and pulled her arms tightly behind her. Officer Hampton ran back down the stairs, passing Ben as he rushed up the last flight. Ben knelt in front of Alex, helping her up and guiding her to the bench. She wiped her tears and her eyes found Billy's. "Did you hear?"

He nodded. "Every word."

Chapter 23

"Maybe I should help her," said the tall man with the lantern jaw.

Alex followed Juke's eyes and saw Evelyn threading her way through the crowd with a tray filled with drinks. William jumped up before Juke could stand and cleared a path for the tiny redhead. "Make way, make way for our she-ro!" he shouted. Alex could barely hear him over the band.

Evelyn set the tray down on the table and began passing around cocktails and beers. "She's the she-ro," she said, putting a rocks glass topped with a cherry and orange garnish in front of Alex.

Phil reached across the table to grab a pint. "Sue told me you pocket dialed Billy and he heard the whole thing." Sue took the other pint and tapped her glass against Phil's.

"I set his number on speed dial and William here told him to expect a call from me," Alex explained.

"I told you all she was brilliant, didn't I?" William returned to his seat and preened over his friend. "Simply brilliant."

Juke stood up and pulled out a chair as Evelyn approached his side of the table. She rolled her eyes at him, but she sat down anyway. "Would you stop that?" she ordered, her smile taking the edge off the words.

"Nope. I will not."

They all laughed, and Alex looked at each of the people at the table. She'd known everyone but William for less than five days, and yet they felt like friends, like family. The band stopped for a break and she glimpsed Georgia and Gabe, her bass player, making their way towards their table. Behind them followed the singer who'd been performing at the gazebo two days before. She watched as he approached, pulling her eyes away only when William elbowed her.

It was hard to believe it had been a mere two days since Deborah had shot Kaine and he'd fallen to his death. She proclaimed her innocence, of course, and said she shot him out of self-defense. When Billy told her to give it up because he'd heard her entire confession, she stated she had confessed nothing; it was all Alex's wild imagination.

That might have caused them all some concern until they got the ballistics report. The gun used to murder Nick was the same gun that had been used to kill Kaine's contractor. The search warrant for Deborah's condo back in Chicago included her computer and her phone, and both were a windfall. She'd be going away for a very, very long time.

Georgia reached the table and turned a chair around, straddling it and resting her arms on the back. Gabe stood at her side and rested his hand on her shoulder. "Told you she'd fix it," Georgia said.

"When you're right, you're right," Phil replied.

Alex had the good grace to blush, but no one other than her, and possibly William, knew it had nothing to do with their compliments and everything to do with the sultry smile of the man with the baritone voice who stood to the other side of Georgia. She hadn't seen him since the quasi-celebration at The Mast, but as she kept eye contact with him, she felt an electric connection.

"And there he is," Sue said, and Alex broke the thread and watched Ben approach.

William whispered in her ear. "I'm not sure it's a good thing he's being rewarded for his obsession with you."

"It's not just that, you know. He was also following Kaine for his story."

"Which he wouldn't have had if he hadn't been stalking you."

He was right, Alex thought. Ben walked over and Evelyn handed him a rocks glass. He waved it off. "Thanks, but I'm heading back tonight. I just wanted to stop in and say goodbye." It was said to the group, but he looked only at Alex.

Evelyn shrugged and kept the drink for herself. "I never heard. Where did you go when those three were inside the restaurant?"

With effort, Ben tore his eyes from Alex to answer Evelyn. "I drove around the block because I thought it was odd that Deborah had parked by a dumpster and decided maybe I should be ready to follow her, especially when the three of them came out together. I knew Alex wouldn't ever voluntarily get in a car with Kaine."

"Billy said you tried to call him while tailing them," William said, "but he was connected to Alex and couldn't hang up."

"He told me. I'm just glad she called him first, and glad he answered." Ben said. "Well, I've got a long drive ahead of me." He turned and started towards the door.

"Ben," Alex said. He stopped. "Thank you." He kept his back to her, nodded, and walked away.

The table kept quiet for a moment. Then William broke the silence. "I don't think that's the last you're going to see of him, Miss Heartbreaker."

Alex smiled sorrowfully. "No, probably not. But for now," she brightened, "I believe we have some celebrating to do."

"Cheers!" they all cried. Evelyn mouthed a thank you to Alex, and then another to William.

Alex closed the door softly behind her and padded across the damp grass to the beach. She gasped as the cold water kissed her toes. Stars twinkled, then slowly disappeared with the sun's arrival. This morning's display featured pastels: lavender, blush, and a pale, pale yellow that was almost white. It was a peaceful start to what would be her last day in Alvin's Landing. She sat in the blue Adirondack chair, her favorite, and breathed in the pine-infused air. She heard a soft swish and looked up to see Evelyn walking towards her, followed closely by Alvin.

"May I?" Evelyn asked, indicating the yellow chair next to Alex.

"Of course. I was hoping to see you before leaving today."

"Here I am," Evelyn smiled, and sat down. Alvin jumped onto her lap and began kneading her thighs. Evelyn absent-mindedly played with his tail. "You know you're welcome back anytime."

"Thank you. I didn't get a chance to ask you last night; what's going to happen with The Mast now that Kaine's gone?"

"It's still ours, Lars and mine," she said. "I found him a treatment center, by the way. He's checking in tomorrow."

"I'm glad he's getting help," Alex said. "Not to be crass, but what about the taxes?"

Evelyn picked up Alvin and set him on the ground, then pulled her knees up to her chin and wrapped her arms around her shins. The cat huffed and walked over to Alex's chair, rubbing against one of the legs. "They'll be paid," Evelyn said, her relief evident. "I didn't know he'd done this, but Nick made up a will after he proposed. He left everything to me. His house is mortgaged to the hilt, but he also took out a rather large life insurance policy, and I'm the beneficiary." She raised her eyes to Alex, and the pain was obvious. "He wasn't all bad."

Alex reached over and patted her shoulder, then scooped up Alvin and put the cat on her lap. "I know. Few people are."

They heard a sliding glass door open and close and turned to see Harriet walking towards them. "Good morning, Harriet," Alex said.

"Good morning, Alexis, er, I mean, Alex."

Evelyn stood up. "I meant what I said," she said to Alex. "Any time."

Harriet watched her walk away and then sat in the chair Evelyn had vacated.

"I didn't know you were a morning person," Alex said.

"I'm not. Trying to be, though. Trying to be a lot of things." Harriet paused. "Look, I wanted to apologize. I didn't know you were so sensitive about your name. I was trying to be, I don't know, chummy? I'm not very good at that," she admitted.

Alex breathed in. This was the last thing she expected. She thought of what she'd just said to Evelyn. Few people were all bad, and that included Harriet.

"Thank you," she said. "I appreciate that, and I'm sorry for blowing up at you the other day."

"It's understandable, considering what you've been through." Harriet paused at Alex's gaze. "My mom had breast cancer. They didn't find it in time."

"Oh. Harriet. I am so sorry."

She shrugged. "It happened a long time ago. Anyway, I just wanted to say I'm sorry and that I'm glad you're okay. Now that you're back, I know we'll be seeing each other more and I don't want it to be like it has been." She blew her hair out of her eyes. "What a week, eh? What a week." Harriet stood up and looked over at the marina. "I'm glad Kaine didn't get this place."

Alex watched Harriet walk back to the patio of her first floor room and open the sliding glass door. *Will wonders never cease?* she thought. The sun crested the horizon. She gave Alvin one last squeeze, put him on the seat of her favorite Adirondack chair, and walked to her room. She planned to take a long hike in the Reserve before packing up and then meeting William for one last basket of cheese curds and a giant small ice cream sundae.

She was back.

Thanks for reading *Peril on the Peninsula*. I hope you enjoyed meeting Alex, William, Evelyn, Juke, and, of course, Alvin. If so, would you consider leaving a review on your favorite platform? It will help other readers meet them, too.

Turn the page for a recipe from The Mast's welcome reception.

Did the passed appetizers at The Mast's opening reception sound tasty? Here's a recipe for the crostini with sirloin, brie, and cherry compote so you can make it yourself.

Crostini with Rosemary Sirloin, Brie, and Cherry Compote

- Crostini
- Brie, sliced
- Rosemary Sirloin
- Cherry Compote

Assemble by topping the crostini with sirloin, brie, and cherry compote. Garnish with a rosemary sprig if you're feeling fancy.

Garlic Grilled Crostini

- Baguette or crusty bread of choice
- Garlic, minced
- Extra-virgin olive oil

Preheat a grill or grill pan to medium-high

Cut the bread into quarter-inch slices

Mix the garlic and olive oil

Brush one side of the bread

Place bread, olive-oil side up, on grill grates or grill pan. Turn after a couple minutes. Watch closely so it doesn't burn.

Keep turning until the bread gets to your desired level of crustiness.

Pro-tip: cook bacon in the grill pan first and you can add some bacon-y goodness to your crostini.

Rosemary Sirloin

- 1lb sirloin or flank steak
- 1tbsp fresh rosemary, chopped
- 2 cloves garlic, diced
- 2 tbsp olive oil
- 2 tbsp balsamic vinegar
- 1 tsp salt

Combine all the ingredients except for the sirloin.

Pour over the sirloin and let sit for thirty minutes to an hour at room temperature.

Heat the grill to high – as in, hot as it can go.

Sear the sirloin, 3 – 4 minutes per side. Longer if you prefer your steaks done to medium or more.

Remove sirloin from heat and let rest at least 5 minutes

Slice thinly against the grain

Cherry Compote

- 24oz pitted sour cherries in light syrup, drained
- 1/2 cup sugar
- pinch ground cinnamon (optional)
- 1 tsp balsamic vinegar, or to taste
- 3/4 teaspoon cornstarch
- 1 tsp water

Bring cherries, sugar, and cinnamon (optional) to a simmer for about ten minutes.

Mash the cherries, if you like.

Stir in balsamic vinegar.

Whisk the cornstarch and water until no lumps remain.

Pour into the pan with the cherries and simmer until sauce thickens.

You can either strain the liquid or let it simmer until the mixture gets a jam-like consistency.

Add more balsamic vinegar to taste.

Author Note

While I set this novel in the very real peninsula of Door County, Wisconsin, the majority of the places mentioned are products of my imagination. There's no Alvin's Landing, The Mast, Rowdy Cormorant, etc. There is a place that serves ice cream sundaes as big as your head, and it does have red and white striped awnings, and it's near a gazebo. If you recognize it, email me and let me know. I'd love to hear from you!

I also made up the people, and any resemblance to real characters is unintentional.

Is Alex Paige me? In some ways, yes. They say write what you know, and as a travel writer and breast cancer survivor, I've certainly followed that dictum. But one thing I now know is that when you write, when you listen to your characters, they take on lives of their own. They become individuals who speak and react in unexpected and often delightful ways. I never knew what was going to come out of William's mouth, and Alex is definitely her own person.

It's been wonderful getting to know them, and I hope you feel the same.

Acknowledgments

I'd wanted to write a novel since I first read a book without pictures. Oh, the magic of being transported somewhere else, some other time, with strangers who became intimate acquaintances, and often felt like friends. I dreamed of performing such magical feats for others.

Took me fifty-one years, cancer, and a global pandemic, but I finally did it. I wrote my first novel.

I began, like so many, by attempting NaNoWriMo - National Novel Writing Month. Every November, novelists and wannabes attempt to pen 50,000 words in thirty days. I didn't, but the challenge got me started. By March, I'd typed *The End*.

Although writing is solitary, I knew I was never alone. My husband, Jim, encouraged me, listened to me ramble about people and places I'd made up, and backed away slowly when I wondered how long it takes someone to die after being stabbed. When I asked him about guns backfiring, he answered seriously. He didn't yawn once one early Saturday morning when I launched into a recap of my entire plot up to that point. He's not a coffee drinker, so he didn't even have that to help him.

Then there are my parents, who are my frontline editors. Mom's grammar and accounting expertise help prevent mistakes (any made are mine, of course). Dad's "tiny little suggestions" and questions about procedure, requests for a better opening, and so many other comments made not-so-tiny improvements. The book is a gazillion times better than if I'd been left to my own devices.

And then, Heidi Kohz. While life got in the way, her initial comments helped me focus.

Marq Withers eased my concerns about a passage I absolutely wanted to get right. Thank you.

Tatiana Abramova, who's edited several of my nonfiction books, is everything a writer wants in an editor, at least everything this one wants: detailed, focused, blunt, wicked smart, and complimentary, when I deserve it. When she says my work is good, I believe her.

To my beta readers: putting Peril in your hands scared me. (Frankly, I was scared to put it in anybody's hands.) What if you hated it? What if you thought it was stupid? What if you thought *I* was stupid? I finally jumped, and you caught me. Some of you had questions, and answering them made the book stronger. Some of you told me you loved it, you thought it was fun, a quick read, an escape—basically everything I was shooting for. Jim and Karen Goodrich (who get an additional shout-out as the best in-laws ever), Karen Gill, Elizabeth McCarthy, Joan Stommen, Sylvia Key, Cindy Ladage, Jessica Waytenick, Shelly Harms, Susan Jarrett, Alicia Underlee Nelson, Lori Helke, Tracy Beyer, Sarah Abrahamson, Lexi Wurpts, Betsi Hill, Sage Scott, April Berry, and Larry Pratt—THANK YOU! (And if I missed anyone, I hope you'll accept my sincere apologies.)

Wait'll you read the next one.

Theresa L. Carter

About Theresa L. Carter

Theresa L. Carter is Theresa L. Goodrich's pen name. It's also her maiden name, the name she had when she dreamed at a tender young age (as most authors do) of writing a novel. While her husband, Jim (who is universally acknowledged as a saint) did not know this at the time of their marriage, it did not influence her decision to stick with Carter for her fiction. (The blame for that rests solely on Amazon's algorithms.)

Theresa is a travel writer and breast cancer survivor who lives in the Chicago area. In her debut novel, she took the "write what you know" maxim to heart and created Alex Paige, a travel writer and breast cancer survivor who lives in Chicago, although she's quick to argue that Alex is definitely her own person.

When Theresa's not traveling, writing, or dreaming about traveling and writing, she likes to cook, read, and decide which bright shiny object she's going to assiduously ignore next.

You can find Theresa on social media @thelocaltourist and at TheLocalTourist.com.

Made in the USA
Middletown, DE
07 August 2022